DESCENT INTO HELL

To Suzy,

This is just

a start —

Reg

DESCENT INTO HELL
in the Land of Human Rights

Written and translated from French by
Régine Mfoumou

Rhema Publications
145-157 St John Street – London EC1V 4PW

DESCENT INTO HELL
Copyright © Régine Mfoumou, 2011

ISBN 978-0-9568487-0-3

First Published in Great Britain in 2011 by Rhema Publications
Rhema Publications Ltd
Suite 15572 - Lower Ground Floor
145-157 St John Street – London EC1V 4PW

Printed in Great Britain by
www.direct-pod.com

To my late father, Josue Mvondo, and to my mother, Sophie Mvondo, whose courage, strength and faith I admire.

Acknowledgements

I want to express my gratitude to all those who encouraged me in fulfilling this publishing project: Paul Zo'obo, Geraldine Jippé and H. E. Adolphus K. Arthur. And for their special assistance in preparing this translation, I would like to thank Nicole Harris, Swain Williams and Kobina Arthur.

I also wish to thank all my friends and family members who helped me with their patience, their trust and love, especially my children Bertrand Arthur, Jules-Aurelien Arthur and Kweku Arthur, my aunt Jacqueline Bernadette Bandolo; and for their unfailing support, Gladys Pennont, Sophie Jippé, my brothers Jean-Jules Minlo and Joseph Effa, and my sister, Chantal Jippé.

« Never allow someone to undermine you to the point of hating them. »
Martin Luther King.

I

At the first light of dawn, the neighbourhood's atmosphere was already filled with exhilaration. Diffused lights and people's outcries launched this unique day. Back home, most parents anxiously await this day as a well-deserved reward for years spent raising their young daughters to the age of marriage. In our culture, it is crucial that a wife gives her husband a daughter, as the continuity of the family line maintained by the male is not enough. From the age of reason, the daughter, a wondrous promise of riches to come, must be taught household chores and therefore be prepared for her future role as a wife and a mother. For example, at the age of nine, my mother used to send me to the market, which was about ten minutes' walk from home, to buy fresh food for the meal of the day. Some mornings, when I was not at school, I stayed in the kitchen to help her. Most afternoons I did not have classes. Therefore I would take part in various improvised household chores or benefit from some jovial playtime with some of the neighbourhood children, if I did not have to attend embroidery or knitting lessons. I would play outside until the return of my father, who did not particularly like the friends I had, as he feared I would copy their bad habits. Shortening these moments I cherished so much always made me very upset because I found it difficult to understand why this inclemency did not apply to my three brothers and my little sister. That was how I grew up: pampered and overly protected by my parents, so much so that, all the way up to my high school years, I was a bit segregated from neighbourhood children and developed no particular friendships.

As for my father, who, many years earlier, left the village to settle in the capital for a better life, marrying off one of his daughters was primarily a matter of honour and consideration towards his family that, in keeping with our custom, was the undeniable warrantor of my future life in a couple. And, even though they never contributed to my education, my suitor was indebted to them for that. At my request, and with regard to his moral obligations to the family, my father promptly visited each of his relatives, as well as their children, inviting them to a meeting. It was such an extraordinary and glorious moment that our little house had to be given a second and exceptional face-lift in order to be ready to host all these guests who would certainly not miss the festivities that would follow the rites of my traditional marriage. Not only was such an occasion, for many of them, especially the women, an opportunity to thoroughly enjoy some large chunks of fleshly slaughtered ox and goat, but also because the men always allowed themselves to be tempted by demijohn palm wine bottles or litres of draught beer. On this occasion, even the oldest ones, worn out by the hands of time and long farming working hours, were temporarily able to recover energy to be present at my wedding, motivated by their secret hope of obtaining supplies of food that were hard to find in the village.

On that fateful day, the whole morning was witness to the unremitting goings and comings of young people commissioned by adults giving orders, criticizing or ensuring the completion of tasks, such as the making of a guard of honour from the palm leaves that surrounded the walls of our home made of rough blocks stacked together with red mud and cement plaster. On the side of our house, two slightly curvaceous girls dressed in brightly coloured cloth were happily planting their pestles at the bottom of the mortar in turn, before raising them cautiously well above their heads without blinking, to ensure no palm nut escapes their vertical crushing. In the backyard, the smoke from the tripod fireplaces set up by my mother, who had appealed to some members of her family for help, was betraying the feast's preparation. The women were very busy keeping up the pace under the discreet supervision of my aunts who were extremely careful to limit the loss of pieces of meat or fish that could disappear under loose dresses hiding plastic bags especially brought for such discreet and mischievous pilfering.

Meanwhile, my father was in charge of hosting the first guests who had braved the steep and unpaved pathway that led to our door. As taxi drivers were unwilling to go up that road, you had to walk for about ten minutes between the crossroads, where most motorists stopped, and our home. The most adventurous could risk taking mototaxis, which were less reassuring because of the number of passengers they carried at a time and the speed at which their drivers rode them just to achieve their cost-effective goal for the day. But for that occasion, my father had requisitioned two young people to operate a shuttle service between the house and the crossroads, carrying family members in his old Peugeot 504 that he generously made available. However, he had taken care to renovate it ahead of schedule, ignoring the car's ordinary cycle of maintenance, which was to routinely paint it every five years. Thus, it was successively transformed from pure white to night black, having already been taxi yellow and earth brown. The latter colour was my father's favourite because he felt that it made the car less visible and camouflaged dirt, allowing him to save on the use of water during the dry season.

At about three o'clock, the chief of my father's village made his entrance into our humble refurbished house. He was preceded by a noisy procession of men and women wearing outfits of various cuts from the same fabric and singing praises to the sovereign while walking in a single file towards our house. All of a sudden, as they were approaching the main door, the songs stopped. The escort broke into two distinct groups that faced each other, while half a dozen masked porters were carrying the chief's throne and walking slowly. The chief himself could hardly be seen since his high and cup-shaped stool had to remain covered until arrival at destination. This was a sign that no one was allowed to address him. As the throne passed by, the now silent escort bowed in reverence to show respect to the chief, who was still not visible. He was brought into our house through the widely opened front door. The throne-carriers knelt down. A tall and stout, mature man got out of the procession, and with respect, reached out to help the chief who sat behind the multi-coloured silk fabric which protected him from the curiosity of onlookers and the assembly's clamour. The chief got off his seat. Immediately, my father drew near him to welcome and lead the way to the space reserved for him in our living room that was modestly decorated and enhanced by hand-made white linens and a handful of wild daisies that had been freshly picked along the steep trail leading to one of the Central Lake's shores, which was about a mile away from home. Once the chief was seated, the members of the family followed one another to greet him while the escorts resumed singing outside.

The presence of the chief made the atmosphere more formal. Indeed, along with the village elders, he had travelled to town to bless my union, as I was the first to bring a white into our family! Because of the great experiences he was known to have had, and the respect he had that knew no boundaries, the chief's presence was a sign of the village's general approval of the union. Moreover, the part of dowry that he was going to receive for the village was, on the one hand, to compensate the whole family for my absence, and on the other hand, to cover the cost of the expenses and sacrifices made to provide education for me. In addition, in keeping with the tradition, my parents were obliged to share this dowry with the entire family, by the mere fact of being consanguineously related. Thus, relatives whom I had never heard of were present that day.

The ceremony had begun at last! My father solemnly explained the purpose of this meeting. First of all, he begged the quiet assembly of people gathered around the chief to forgive him for having failed to satisfy the prior introduction of the fiancé to the family. He highlighted the unusual nature of my marriage with his future white son-in-law by trying to restate my own words as much as possible. The congregation was all ears, so he tried to make himself even more audible at times, as his voice had become hoarse due to the chattering and the tension associated with the preparations. He cut his speech short to let the village eldest, as well as the village chief, speak too. Both men asked for palm wine. The chief's stoutest servant was responsible for bringing the drink forth to the ruler because nobody else was allowed to serve him during official ceremonies or without having been initiated. Answering my parents in unison, both dignitaries copiously glorified them and consecrated me as a goddess. Then, they poured wine on the ground as an offering to our dead ancestors, so they could take part in the festivities. Following these preliminaries, the women served the meal. With large plates of food balanced on their heads, they walked one after the other and laid the food in the middle of the family circle. Shortly after being informed by my mother that all the food was brought out to the assembly, my father invited the chief and the village eldest to bless the meal. Then, everyone could drink and eat to their contentment. Finally, the closest members of the family received gifts as a souvenir of my tradi-

tional wedding: kitchen utensils for women, pecuniary enve-
lopes or cans of red wine for men. At the end of the day, the
most tired returned home while the fence of leaves hid young
bingers dancing until going into a trance to the sounds of
balafons that were alternated with the exhaled tunes of the
timeworn speakers of a hi-fi system borrowed for the whole
evening to enable the balafon players to rest their athletic
arms. The same, tripe soup, meat kebabs or grilled fish, all
washed down with an immoderate quaffing of beer, kept the
energetic night owls going until the morning, when they also
started returning home, reluctantly.

Meanwhile, from a thousand miles away, melancholy and
remorse were controlling each of my sighs. Unable to hold
back my tears, I withdrew into myself with a tormented spirit
caused by the distant sweet scent of grilled fish on a soft-
wood-fired stove and the reminiscence of the sugary fragrance of fried banana plantains trying to override the uncon-
tainable smell of game stew. The wonderful memories of the
dowries I had attended made me sad because the folkloric
staging of this unavoidable traditional marriage always led to
an exceptional performance: the young suitor, along with his
parents and the dignitaries of his family, meets the relatives
of the beloved young lady for endless discussions and overtly
asks for her hand; and, in most cases, the request is approved.
This, at the same time, enthrones his fiancée as his eternal
promise. Like most young girls, I had often imagined the
moment when the brothers and sisters of my beloved suitor
would carry me on their shoulders, running, and spurred by
the roaring audience, take me to my new family, while my
eyes shining with emotion would contemplate my mother's
rangy silhouette fading out. Sometimes, the thought of that
separation froze my blood, but the spectacular atmosphere of
that exceptional day always led me to dream. Back home in-

deed, the scope of customary marriage exceeds that of civil marriage which the elders mainly view as a non-formal act imposed by the whites during colonization. Therefore, the dowry has a huge impact on our families, because it alone determines the future of the marriage.

Fresh in my memory was the misfortune a young man underwent ten years earlier, after presenting himself before our extended family to express his desire to marry one of my cousins. He was given a staggering list of goods and victuals by his future in-laws after consultation with their peers. Born into a rather poor family, the young suitor struggled to get as many essential items as possible to offer in exchange for the hand of his bride-to-be. The day came. The young man arrived with only two thirds of the list's requirements for lack of sufficient means, but with the promise to present the remaining third when he could. His future family-in-law had naturally called their relatives together to discuss the modest dowry. So, the usual preliminaries due to the girl to marry began. But, when the time came to proceed to the exchange, the representative of the young man's family apologized for the missing two goats and one pressure cooker. Even though nobody interrupted him, the sceptical eyes of my cousin's parents turned towards the assembly expressing their uncompromising refusal. The unfortunate allegory of their agreement would have significantly condemned their daughter to become *the cheapest one* in her future family-in-law because she would have lost her dignity and respect during her dowry, not only as a result of her bargain, but also because her parents would have been contented with the very few possessions presented against her traditional wedding, and above all, on credit! Thus, when the man finished his speech, our family's elders gathered to one side, and then came in front of the assembly a few minutes later. Their spokesman disclosed the verdict: they were accepting the goods and the other few offerings, but their daughter would not leave their village on credit! His firm tone and his tightened face distinctly extinguished the joy previously displayed by the welcomed family. Now, disappointed, the even more determined suitor and his family left empty-handed, after having attended the naturally dull festivity that followed the aborted traditional rite.

My cousin was able to move to her husband's home only nine months later, once the dowry was completed, her parents entirely satisfied and the village abundantly replete, since the second ceremony was fulfilled in line with our traditional rules, occasioning a party and joyful dancing once more. And, as the unpredictable was always common during such celebrations, and I knew it very well, I was slightly anxious, mainly because in my case, our customs were distorted by my absence, my fiancé's absence, and above all, by my real condition, solitude and the lie undermining my spirit which was deeply embroiled in the weight of my daily routine. A disgrace! Terrified by uncertainty, I lost appetite and sleep: the destiny of my life in a couple was in the hands of the family assembly. And, as the event was moving forward back home, my unstable disposition was increasing. After a period of monotonous boredom, I regained courage and called my only comfort, my mother.

II

Many whites had already approached me over the Internet. Then came George, who changed my destiny. Endless hours in front our computers, answering our emails or scrutinizing our respective pictures, when we did not express our bursts of love over the phone, such were our weekly dates.

George and I had been communicating over the Internet for about two years. I had spent long hours in front of a computer screen in a cybercafé, most often admiring and daydreaming when looking at his pictures, which fuelled our discussions on the telephone and strengthened my feelings. Thus, whenever I was writing long emails to him, I always tried to embellish them with sweet words that my penfriend seemed to like, so he also tried to answer me with a passion he never failed to stress when we talked on the phone. Our regular telephone dates became so important for me that I eagerly expected his calls, excited and cheerful, like a child on Christmas Eve. He brightened up my days with his deep but caring voice, always arousing great hope in me. It was probably a habit, but the strength of our growing connection gradually took away the virtual character of our relationship. We became close. So close, that we felt we had known each other for a long time; subsequently, George was seized by the instinct for discovery. Eventually, the trip he made, braving the distance and everything against us, to come and visit me in Cameroon. Upon his arrival, he was very generous, which made a strong impression on my family.

His visit was an unexpected festive occasion that precipitated my parents to use the annuities from their various tontine loans in order to whitewash our home's rough walls of concrete block that were dirtied by the reddish-brown dust of cars driving through during arid days of the dry season. Likewise, to honour him, my bedroom took advantage of this timely refurbishing to enhance itself with new drapery and the only mosquito net of our house. George would soon come from Paris. The news spread in the neighbourhood from mouth to mouth, so fast, that within two days, all ears had heard about it. I found it now impossible to take a step without being stopped. Everyone wanted to be better informed than others concerning my guest's visit. Some of my friends who regularly went to the cybercafé in search of a marriageable white nicknamed me Georgina or Mrs. George. Frankly, I was delighted, because it brought me closer to my virtual love who was shortly going to appear before me in flesh and bone.

Mixed apprehension and impatience kept me awake all night before the arrival of George. The day seemed endless. His plane was meant to land on the airport runway late in the afternoon. Before going there, in the company of my parents, my younger brothers, my sister and a few friends, I had coddled myself, trying to bring my appearance to perfection at the beauty salon where my hair was drawn up and tightly shaped in the form of a banana at the front part of my head, thus clearing my forehead properly so as to highlight the eyeliner's light line that replaced my over-plucked eyebrows, my thickened eyelashes, and the pearly eye-shadow that intensified my glowing expression; shortly before that, I had picked up the wax-fabric gown the seamstress had crafted from a model seen in La Redoute catalogue. My parents were undoubtedly more nervous than I was. They were trying to entertain us with speeches and anecdotes in order to divert our attention from our pressing impatience: the flight's delay. Finally, the thunderous noise of the 747-Combi's tyres on the landing strip drew a sense of palpable excitement on our faces. Soon after, passengers began to appear without haste, through the highly controlled customs gates. I was staring at them one by one, with inquisitive and insistent eyes, more particularly every white man who came out. In next to no time, George showed up, dragging a large suitcase behind him.

I recognized him first. I had repeatedly received pictures of him, of his apartment, his car and his cat. I had studied all of them thoroughly, so I had the feeling that George was familiar, and especially the lack of pomp in his daily routine seemed to suggest a simple life with no secrets. Consequently, I was very surprised to find out how short he was as no picture he had sent me had led me to suspect it. Seeing his joyous face made my disappointment vanish in an instant, as he shaped a large smile when his eyes finally met mine while I was walking in his direction; meantime euphoria seized all my partners who assailed him with embraces, each one trying to draw his attention. Through short words uttered shyly, my guest tried to answer these marks of affection he did not understand immediately. His eyes were constantly looking for me, as if to find the strength to face this surprise crowd that he apparently did not expect.

The first moments were followed by extensive presentations. Afterwards, we headed off in search of taxis to go home. A slight confusion marked the moment, since no one in my escort had enough money to pay for their return trip. Everyone being financially limited, my parents first, and nobody being willing to admit they had money for their taxi fees, George felt compelled to pay the price of general transportation. I was obviously embarrassed and apologized to my host whose spontaneous generosity was, much more than any thankfulness, greatly appreciated throughout his stay.

At home, my friends resentfully shortened their presence to let us get to know our new guest. It was George's first trip to Africa. His eyes, which followed each of my movements, made me understand that he did not want me to leave him with the others, not even my parents. I was particularly amazed by his reserve and the slight apprehension that made him as sensitive as a child. George, in flesh, at home! I did not immediately feel the vibration of love at first sight, but I sensed I had finally found the man of my dreams.

My mother served the grilled mackerel and peanut sauce she had prepared that morning and set aside for George's first dinner at home. I wanted to add a Western-style mixed salad to the menu, but my parents were strongly opposed to it, as they believed that food was an effective way of judging an individual's adaptability, particularly that of a stranger. Sure they were right, I changed my mind and I instantly placed a dozen plums in a saucepan over gentle heat to soften their skin and reduce the bitterness of their raw flesh.

George had a clear preference for the fish, even though its spicy seasoning made him a bit uncomfortable. But, being very courteous, he made a point to taste all the food on the table, which pleased us. His ability to adapt to our ways in the first hours erased the preconceived ideas produced by the organization of his visit. My parents were also delighted and whispered that his natural ease made him a good man. Their appraisal was reinforced shortly after dinner, when, without being embarrassed, he went into the enclosure marked by the boundary of the corrugated iron sheets nailed to wooden stakes driven into the ground, which housed our privy, lit by the trembling wick of a hurricane lamp.

After a night of contemplation and mutual discovery, still feeling weary because of his long journey, George did not get up at dawn. I preceded him to help my mother with morning labours. To save the power of our antiquated stove, my mother set up the fire behind the house, where she placed a large pot of water. The atmosphere was less electric than the previous day. Time passed slowly, our regular activities progressed as normal until everyone else at home woke up. When George came out of my bedroom, the house had already resumed its usual aspect of this time of day, dim and cold, waiting for the heat generated by the sharing of doughnuts, beans and hot porridge purchased at the street corner a few minutes earlier. After greeting my parents, I walked my guest down to the bathhouse, warmed by the first rays of sun. His towel hanging on his shoulder and a block of soap in hand, he found the trench framed by two wooden plates that we used as our latrines. I helped him to hang his towel on a nail knocked in one of the stakes. A large bucket of warm water was already waiting for him. Obviously ill-at-ease, I let him take a shower, after strongly advising him to close the metal sheet door with the block of bond stone placed near the bucket, otherwise, it would open and expose him, naked, to passersby. My warning amused him. He smiled as he was closing the gate. Before walking away, I reminded him not to leave anything in the latrine after bathing, including the bucket and soap. Behind me, I heard low-flow tap tap tap drops of water falling on the thin corrugated and rusty metal plates surrounding the toilets.

A few minutes later, while sitting on a stool at the entrance of the house, I saw George resurfacing, the bucket and soap in his hand, the towel hanging over his left shoulder. The brightness of his white bathrobe securely fastened around his waist illuminated his face. His shoulder-length hair had flattened from his forehead to the neck, revealing his big ears. The expression on his oval face was revived and radiant. I watched him walking towards me, in the already shining light of the rising day, and I realized how different... white he was. It filled me with pride and a spontaneous smile appeared on my lips. He handed me the bucket. I took it and told him that we actually shared the latrines with all the nearby inhabitants. The disappearance of anything forgotten was commonplace, and had brought about conflicts between several neighbours in the past.

Once dressed, George joined my father in the dining room where they had breakfast together. My mother had already gone to the market, leaving me to take care of them and act as an interpreter. My father was always speaking in parables. So I had to simplify his words to George who was speaking fast, with an accent that forced my father to request the repetition or translation of whatever he had said, which I did, translating either into French or into our language. George showed some cordial ease, thus enabling us to quickly break down the barriers of the unknown, so we soon found ourselves making plans for his stay.

The first visit we made was to the town centre. Before the dazzling sun of midday, aboard a yellow cab hired for the day, we drove through the narrow streets swarming with all kinds of vehicles, and among newer buildings and the last vestiges of European settlers that were damaged by ignorant vandals. Our capital also showed George its countless children as well as its young vendors carrying bowls on their heads and illegally selling to passersby, to tourists or those who were going to work: peeled oranges, papayas or pineapples, salted peanuts, or even ginger juice and other refreshments were exchanged for one or two coins. We briefly stopped at the main post office into town. George bought two postcards on which he wrote a quick little note before posting them. This gave us the opportunity to make an initial purchase of those tempting fruits. After that, we returned to the car. The driver dropped us home just in time for lunch.

George, my parents and I ate at the table, while my four younger siblings contented themselves with benches in the kitchen and used their knees to support their plates. George's eyes showed that he did not understand that setting aside of part of the family. Before he asked the question, I told him that children were not allowed to sit down at the table with adults when we had guests, out of respect, to allow them to talk freely. He looked as if puzzled but said nothing. When the meal was over, my father went to his bedroom, as his daily two-hour nap could not be overlooked, after jokingly reminding my mother that it was forbidden to wake him up, except in case of serious illness or death. Meanwhile, the visit of one of my friends encouraged George to stay with us. We both spent part of the afternoon chatting and informing George of everything people had said about me and him well before his arrival. He was relaxed and much amused to hear all the praise about him in the neighbourhood. Finally, we decided to take him out for a stroll.

George soon realized that we had told him the truth: everyone seemed to know him and called him by his first name. He was waved or smiled here and there. Courteous, he pleasantly responded, then looked at me, hoping to read endorsement in my eyes. My friend and I showed him the café where I wrote to him as well as the phone shop where I used to wait for his monthly calls. I was filled with emotion and nervously reminded him that our meeting would not have been possible without these places, because my family could not afford a computer, or the Internet subscription. As we walked towards the hair salon where I often killed the never-ending days, I explained to him all the sacrifices my father had made by providing me with weekly finances for me to communicate with him as often as I wished. His compassionate voice expressed some deep gratitude. Finally, our steps led us up to my father's shop, just before it closed, so we helped him by storing ill-positioned items and sweeping the floor. When we finished, we took leave of my friend and went back home along with my father. Thus, George was able to observe my monotonous routine within a single day.

After several days, George felt quite at ease to stay home with my mother when I had to be absent a few hours or go to the market. One morning, I went to the shop to help my father out. Two friends of mine visited our home. My mother was preparing the lunch and George was settled in the dining room where he was vainly trying to get a fix on the waves of my father's temperamental and sizzling international radio. When he saw them, he greeted them like the householder. They sat with him and deceitfully got him involved in a discussion about life in France, our country and their unrealistic aspirations to be in the West: one wanted money to invest in the trade of fresh fish and seafood between the coast and the capital, but opportunities to find the funds required to start a small business were as rare as meeting a European benefactor like him; the other who was more ambitious, hoped to leave the country through the unexpected kindness of a white man whose generosity would enable her to achieve her dreams. Eventually, their subtle grievances ended with a warning that George could not hide from me when I came back: the two termagants had advised him not to trust me because I maintained a longstanding relationship with another man. Well prepared to sow doubt in George's mind, they seemed, according to him, as surprised as him when they revealed the sarcastic news that was going to spread confusion and now disturbed my guest, despite the fact that he had never seen anything unusual since his arrival. However, his eagerness to get to the bottom of the matter now urged him to enquire whether my repeated morning outings were not in fact a pretext to meet up with that other man. Despite my explanation, his unfortunate deduction involved my parents in the league of what he called a disgraceful deception, which saddened me deeply. I finally understood why George had left the dining room to lock himself in the bedroom since the departure of the two young ladies. His eyes staring at the ceiling, he tried to wipe out paper over the cracks of the unacceptable and humiliating revelation, so much that he wished he was far from us: my effective absences, my private conversations with my parents in our dialect or my deafening laughter when talking in the kitchen with my mother... these uncountable sardonic scenes now made him sick. He no longer wished to see or talk to any of us.

In fact, my mother was the first to tell me about the visit of my so-called friends. She insisted on the fact that George had remained in their company for a long time, alone! I immediately felt anger in my guts, but I could not scream. Both, inseparable from their bad language, had caused much damage around the neighbourhood since I had known them. Their infringements had unscrupulously broken households or sowed discord, for the sole purpose of earning the interest and attention of the unfortunate male whom one of them had set her cap at. When she said that George had been barricaded in his room since their departure, I understood! Very happily, the shrews had had enough time to pour their venom upon him.

I explained to George that I indeed used to have a relationship that had stopped long before he decided to visit me, and that from the very moment I understood our relationship was serious, after his promise to come and see me, I had not allowed myself to date anyone else. But all in vain, for he continued to feel deeply betrayed throughout the remaining time of his stay. The playful rapport we had from the first moments he spent at home completely vanished. And, to avoid the discomfort of heavy silences and courteous glances from each other, George preferred the comfort provided by our walks. Once, we went into town to buy souvenirs since he especially liked the market. We often stopped there for the pleasure of seeing him bargain with the traders who impulsively doubled their prices when they noticed that the colour of his skin was less tanned than the few whites who regularly circulated in the vicinity of the French supermarket, which we entered one day out of curiosity. George had bought a few apples there, despite my efforts to deter him because their price seemed excessive compared to what we might have spent in an open-air market.

Far from his usual comfort, George was forced to adapt to the leisurely pace of our life without artifice. However, this change of scenery was invigorating for him because it brought him back to the essence of a ageless life where humanity still prevailed over machines, where patience and indulgence replaced the dictatorial rush of a timed life that he experience in his country: no more notion of time; everywhere, everyday habits governed the time. For the first time in his life, he saw the time pass, calmly, despite the irreparable confusion that now sullied the memory of our encounter.

After spending two weeks in my family, George returned to France unknowingly leaving me to manage all sorts of comments that I did no longer answer. Whether envious or considerate, some people in my neighbourhood could not refrain from expressing their opinions in their own way about the visit of "the white" who was soon going to help me escape from the life without prospects we were subjected to. Yet, that brief encounter had only enabled me to make contact with George. As usual, I never replied to the supporters of the shrews who were striving, better than me, to spread the details of George's stay. Only my closest friends, three in number, were in on the secret: George had suggested that another meeting would not be possible, because he was not earning enough money to afford to travel to Africa as much as he would have hoped. Similarly, he could not afford to welcome me to France and, in any case, he was no longer sure of anything. Nonetheless, he promised to write as often as in the past. His honesty touched me. Subsequently, I became very thoughtful towards him as if he needed that to believe in my sincerity. Still, in my heart, an indescribable burden remained, which continually reminded me that my secret hopes were forever swept away. Until the end of his stay, we still tried to enjoy every moment, now aware of the reality of our quite different lifestyles.

Two long weeks had passed since George's departure. I was without news of him. I then presumed that the revulsion instilled in his mind by doubt had prevailed over the truth. Finally, my efforts to reassure him had proved useless; frustration and repressed anger started growing inside me whenever I thought of his visit. Some days I even had deep regrets. Other times, I got angry at myself because I had not been able to anticipate such slanderous acting when I was well aware of the *kongossa* that fuelled some people's life in our neighbourhood, and who, for lack of projects or ambition had sabotaged others daily. My uncontrollable murmurs verbalized my inner turmoil; they became regular and unpleasant, urging my mother to advise me to keep my composure. She also wished that I could forget George, since his reaction revealed his immaturity. She also thought it was better to realize it at this stage. Moreover, as she believed in predestination, she told me that if George had really been the man of my dreams, he would not have listened to my so-called friends because they were strangers to him. So I promised to follow her advice, which I knew would be with more torment than pleasure. Thus, determined to accept one of the sorrows brought about by life, I steadily resumed my routine, giving my days their ordinary rhythm.

Three weeks after talking with my mother about George, I had to admit she was right, especially as the echo of the white man who had come to spend a good time with me was setting people talking around the neighbourhood. When I was not forced out, I preferred the loving and forbearing shelter of our home, the only place sparing me the unkindness of the gossips my relative called jealousy. Even the cybercafé had become hostile because all the looks, from the regulars to the manager, froze on me whenever I entered to check my email, so that after five exasperating minutes, I always left, escorted by the ironic comments of their familiar mouths. However, despite being an ordinary client at the hair salon for many years, my new nickname, 'the white's wife', had quite favourably cast me among the privileged, except that it was not financially advantageous: now the owner wanted to do my hair personally and her apprentices always expected a tip at each of my visits; nobody wanted to believe that I did not have a penny, because it was inconceivable that my white had not opened an adequately supplied bank account for me.

One morning I woke up in a good mood. I could not explain this feeling. In fact, shame within me seemed to have been pushed away. It was like one of those days when nature brightens the heart unexpectedly. I began a major clean up, as if we were preparing for a celebration at home. I sang one song after another, without being able to prevent it. My radiant face was shining with empathy. I had not experienced such an ardour for several weeks. When I finished cleaning the house, I went to the cybercafé. On the way, holding my head high, I invariably smiled to the mockers inclined to sarcastic disdain since George had left me. Also, at the cybercafé, I faced my detractors with my much assured enthusiasm and silence. George had written to me, finally! My secret hope was instantly rekindled. I read this email, a doubled bundle of joy, although it was not addressed to me directly, but to my parents:

Dear family,
Now that I am back in Paris, I resumed my habits, my work and my small apartment. Ordinarily, one might expect to live it all with joy, because everyone is happy to go back to their nest. This time, this rule only seems to be an illusion as a void has surrounded me since my return. I must say that my stay in your family has done me much good. This trip, which initially was not entirely justified, found its raison d'être once I was in your home where I found a treasure I never thought I would see in my life. Yes, your way of life is so real, sincere, that one wonders: "How can you live elsewhere?"

I do not think it necessary to tell you how touched I was, pleased with the hospitality and the conversations I could have with one another, sometimes finding myself unworthy of such attention.

I wanted to thank you all individually but I would not have had enough time to do so. You form a unit and I think having the opportunity to express my gratitude to the head of the family is enough for all. May God give me a long life to enable us to live through such simple but so beautiful moments again, which were sometimes marked by long silences. The silence that is sometimes more eloquent than words... and say as much as our eyes, because as you know, we come from societies where everything is not said, even if everything is known.

As a man of respect and decency, I tried to hold back what everyone knew or saw. Nevertheless, whatever the gesture or glance, all this was done with the utmost respect for your family. May God guide me! The word family finally has a new meaning for me.

The simplest words being the best, I'll only say: thank you!
Affectionately,
George

I brought this letter home in haste. It had more effect than my success in the Baccalaureate Probationary Test a few years earlier. My parents read much into it and concluded that George was unassumingly asking for my hand. The morning receipts of my father's shop were turned into charitable money early in the afternoon, when it was used to purchase beverages offered to our curious neighbours who were drawn to our door by our overjoyed cheers. Later on, we sat down as a family and my father hastened to warn me to behave myself, because he would do everything possible to encourage George to let me travel as quickly as possible. For that, he was ready to go into debt if George was willing to welcome me. In fact, my opinion did not matter. And, I was not opposed to the idea of joining George because I had got to know him through our countless emails, his very few phone calls, and his stay that had brought us together all the same. Therefore, leaving my country and my neighbourhood? What a dream for all the young people I knew! There was no hesitation: if my destiny would be changed thanks to George, then I was lucky to have met such a kind and generous gentleman. Previously, the delicacy of his sincere tone at the time of our separation had contained a note of regret and desolation when we said goodbye. At present, his obvious affection for my family was a sign that I was entirely free to love him even more. Away with our past misunderstandings, the silences and the distance: George had taken the time to think and had returned to me through this letter. That was enough for me.

In the following days, my correspondence with George was given a boost, becoming more regular now that my parents helped to stimulate our relationship by giving me money every day to go to the cybercafé or to call him. Thus, seven months came and went slowly and smoothly, until George promised me that I would travel to him: he thought we would save time and lose less money that way, because his phone calls were becoming increasingly frequent since my father had sacrificed some of his business monthly income to offer me the only mobile phone in the house to avoid me running to the cybercafé to wait for the phone calls of 'your white' as people there named him.

Three months later, George sent me the money and necessary documents for my visa application, validating the promise made to my father when they spoke to decide about my journey. Without stating special conditions, my father only asked him to watch over me, which George guaranteed to do with all his heart. I immediately began preparing for my impending trip, and keeping information away from prying eyes and ears. I managed to get an entry visa to France for ninety days. Once again, it was another occasion for rejoicing in my family. However, as my departure loomed, my parents preferred to celebrate my visa behind closed doors, to avoid stirring up jealousy, especially because we still had in mind the sudden and tragic death of a local young man who was found dead a few days before flying off to Canada where he was to continue his university studies after obtaining an international grant. For several weeks, the mystery of his death generated debate in the market place, and around the vicinity. Jealousy, greed, and of course witchcraft were suspected as the motives for the crime. Inspired by distrust, as naturally expected, my parents strongly advised me not to tell anyone about my forthcoming trip, which materialized about two weeks after my visa and my reception of the plane ticket sent by George.

All my family was convinced of the wonders of Providence. While my father was blessing the Lord for the white prodigal son He had sent him to get his home out of misery and the mockery he had suffered from his own brothers who despised his efforts to create a profitable trade, my mother spent her time giving me her final recommendations: I had to behave as a good wife to my future husband whom she did not name; I should not forget that my brothers and my sister would remain behind me back home; and, obviously it was very important not to neglect my duty as a child to those who gave me life, nurtured me until my twenty-seventh year and enabled me to know the extraordinary destiny that awaited me now.

I felt no anxiety regarding my journey. George's reassuring words had broken all the fears inspired by the unknown. Furthermore, the impression he had made on my family was so deep that his praises were regularly sung to me since his email to my parents. Instead, I was boiling with impatience because I had never been in an aircraft. And, above all, I was going to *Mbeng*, the European Eldorado... a dream coming true! I wanted to shout it out from the roof of our house or to my friends, but especially to the legion of critics whose itch was inflamed by gossips and the desire to know what was happening with George. For that reason, a few days before leaving, I avoided talking to whoever questioned me about George, remaining rather elusive for fear that my inner joy would unconsciously let words out of my mouth. This contrasting attitude did fuel slanders and accusations in my neighbourhood. Some people claimed that George had married and I did not hear from him anymore, while others even claimed that, at first glance, they knew he was just a petty player of no talent, an opportunist who came to spend quality time with an African! I endured all those comments without replying, assured of my imminent victory and, more importantly, the surprise that I reserved for those criticizing me in their hearts.

The day of my departure came much sooner than I thought. The day before, I shared up almost all my clothes between my sister and two of my friends whom I informed the very same day of my impending adventure. They stayed with me until I took one last glance at the crowded streets of the neighbourhood, before climbing into the taxi that was to drive me to the airport. For my friends it was not only about saying goodbye to me: I became a revered and envied character, to the extent that each of them wanted to ensure they would not be forgotten. But for my parents, our separation did not have to be a sad moment. On the contrary, my mother wept for joy, given that my absence from her home was necessarily occasioning a new hope for a better life. For us, going to France was inevitably synonymous with social development and, consequently, fewer problems. Mostly, this meant I was integrating into the growing generation of Western Union's elite, which made me feel extremely honoured to be the one that would support my family financially. Consequently, I took the plane without hesitation, towards Paris.

III

George had promised to pick me up at Roissy Charles-de-Gaulle airport. He had not provided further details regarding the organization of my stay. I tried to imagine the exciting moment when warm hugs, contagious joviality and tactless curiosity would seal my meeting with him, along with his family and friends, upon my arrival at the airport. All this made me very impatient. Moreover, I had never travelled long distances other than the one between the capital and my village, or the trips I often did in bush taxis when we needed some supplies of game and other products from my family's farms, when the plane landed, the landscape I saw before me was hallucinating. By itself, the airport was as big as my native city. I took a deep breath. A slight smile shaped my lips because the picture of my homecoming came to my mind: large suitcases full of designer clothes which had the sweet scent of France and, finally, the *starwoodian* reception of my family and my friends in whom I would raise all sorts of daydreams owing to my ascent into the elite circle of people who had lots of riches and lived in such luxury that one would have thought their money multiplied as they spent it. In the space of a minute, I directed my nose one last time to my custom-made outfit, which I already undervalued. The sharp smell of oil from the dressmaker's old sewing machine was so encrusted in it that it took me back to the reality of a world I felt I no longer belonged to. I was in Paris! And, despite being used to seeing a few white tourists in town, now, white men and women came and went in all directions, unconcerned, walking fast as to beat the time, so that the number of Blacks that were aboard the plane that had brought us quickly became trifling. Customs formalities completed, and having checked-in no luggage because my carry-on suitcase was more than enough for the five garments I had kept, I found myself outside rather hurriedly, looking for George.

Some passengers who had travelled on the same plane as me were now embracing relatives or friends and heading towards doors that I assumed would lead them to the airport exit. After half an hour, some of those passengers had left the scene. Visibility became clearer. No sign of George. Inside my purse was a notebook where I kept his phone number because my father naturally grabbed the mobile phone he had offered me. Also in my pocket was the only twenty euro note my parents had given me before we parted, when they handed me to the Lord and prayed to Him to allow the note to be multiplied by tens, or even hundreds. I saw a young black lady who was waiting for a passenger and drew near her to asked her to help me make a call to the number I showed her. She kindly accepted and dialled the number on her own cell phone, which she held out to me. The answering machine announced George's absence. When handing back the phone to its owner, she told me to be patient because the person who was coming to pick me up could be stuck in the traffic that often occurred at that time of the day. Relieved to hear that, I walked to the first vacant seat I saw a few steps away.

I kept watching the passengers getting out, meeting someone they knew, rejoicing in their reunion and leaving. My plane had landed more than an hour ago. In my mind, growing anxiety made its way, conceding to fear. For the second time, I walked towards the first black lady my eyes fell on, convinced she would be willing to help me in this foreign land, because her face and elongated size reminded me of the Fulbe back home. She gave a slight backward movement with a suspicious look when I approached her. Although I was very surprised by this attitude, I asked for her help after explaining my situation. She allowed me to phone on her device while holding it until the answering machine set off. Already troubled by George's delay, the distrust of the lady provoked my unexpected coward stuttering, to the extent that I left George a very confusing message. Noticing my discomfort, the lady told me in a more cordial tone that the airport was very far from Paris and my friend must actually be caught in traffic jams. Similarly, she advised patience as a cure for my underlying nervousness. Somewhat comforted by these words, but less than those of the previous lady's, I returned to the seat and continued to stare at passersby.

My notebook was still in my hand, so I began to leaf through it, because I was now thinking of other penfriends I could contact. I also had an envelope containing various letters that one of my friends had given me for a relative living in France. She had taken care to include a phone number. But could I call strangers who were not aware of my arrival? Besides, when my relationship with George took a serious turn, I stopped writing to my white correspondents. Could I turn up at someone's house and be welcomed without embarrassment? Should I call my friend back home first to ask her to beg her cousin to accommodate me temporarily? In my pocket, twenty Euros! In my mind, a series of equations to be solved: at home, I could rent a studio flat for a month with part of that money and feed myself properly with the other, here, would I have enough to make a phone call and get to the place where I would be hosted in the meantime? Why had George not come as planned? What was happening? He could not have helped me obtain the visa and bought an expensive ticket to abandon me this way, in the middle of nowhere, without any familiar sight. Something must have happened to him, but how would I know? Now, I was panic-stricken, trying to think of a way out of this unexpected situation. Suddenly, a distant, panting voice called out "Yvette!" He was calling me, finally! He ran towards me. The anxiety that had gained upon me so pressingly immediately vanished when I saw him.

George came up to me drenched in sweat. He could hardly speak and had to sit a few minutes to regain his strength. During this time he was holding my hand as if to console me for the anxiety produced by his delay. His gesture was very touching, so I did not need any explanation, instead I savoured the moment. George was as pleased as I could be after the oppressive doubt that had somewhat cooled the joy I had imagined about our reunion.

We left the airport without further delay, through various corridors that led us into a strange basement where I was both worried and stunned to see its abounding animation. We took the first train. George explained that his car was too worn out and it could not drive from his home to the airport. It made no difference to me since I was in France, under his providential hands! After more than half an hour, the train stopped at a large crowded station. People were travelling in all directions so that the hubbub of the zealous walking pace mixed with loud conversations marked a sharp contrast with the whispers I had discreetly observed in the first coach we had got in a few minutes earlier. I was particularly struck by the flow of Blacks, some strolling casually, others, mostly young, standing in groups here and there, looking idle, which reminded me of those among us whose only daily activity was drinking beers in the bars where, upon awakening, they tried to transform the world in one day to finally realize that nothing had changed by the evening except their progress towards drunkenness. This vision made me feel a twinge in my heart, because I immediately thought about the families of these young people who had certainly remained in Africa, and had probably placed all their hope in them, as mine had on me now. I could not avoid thinking of the grief my parents would feel if I let them down. My father's recommendations urged me to always listen to my guide, George, due to the dedication and altruism he had shown us through his attitude. Therefore, he expected perfect obedience and behaviour from me towards his future son-in-law. Also, lost in this new haven, with my father's voice echoing in my head, I followed George through the long corridors that led us to a platform where we took another train to his home.

After an hour's ride or so, we finally got to George's accommodation. A two-bedroom apartment in the west suburb of Paris, located on the third floor of a small modern building. From the entrance was a long corridor leading directly into a large room that I assumed to be the main room. In the left corner, I saw the armrest of a sofa and a black chair forming what I thought to be the lounge; in the centre stood a lacquered rattan table under which a few bottles of wine and liquors lined up, touching the floor. The dining table, a small desk on which a computer sat and a shelf on which some books were neatly sorted were all squeezed into the right corner. George invited me to sit on the couch, but being curious, I preferred to look around the rest of the apartment. He then showed me the bathroom and kitchen on one side of the corridor, and on the other, the half-open door of the bedroom lit by the low sunlight of the wonderful spring day, where I could see his big cat intimidated by my presence lying on the bed. I was quickly chilled by the coldness of the flat because it reminded me of the chill produced by the leaves of trees in the evening in my village. Intrigued, I first tried to determine its origin, because within my flesh and my clenched limbs, I kept shivering. The apartment was meticulously equipped, but I was a bit apprehensive because it lacked life. I endeavoured not to show George my anxiety to avoid upsetting him, all in vain. Could it be the lack of humanity behind the closed doors of the building that chilled my blood like that? I finally told myself that the distance from my country and my landmarks could actually explain this strange state, because I now found myself in a new territory, with a stranger as my only resource. I depended entirely on him. Nevertheless, George had noticed my prevailing unease and took great pains to make me feel at ease. He grabbed my hand to lead me to his living room, he made me sit on his little sofa bed, tenderly, and then he went into the kitchen to get the meal ready while he was asking all sorts of questions about my family "down there".

He promised me that I would quickly get used to this new life and he would help me to integrate by teaching me to live in the French way; I should not worry because he was there for me. As I found it strange that there was still no sign of anybody from his family since we had arrived in his apartment, I asked him if people did not come to greet the guests as they did in my country, reminding him of the welcome we had given him during his stay at home. He replied that, little by little, I would meet his parents and his sister, and some friends. He also explained that people did not go to others' homes as he had seen in my country without advance notice, because everyone was always very busy with their work or their problems. In addition, he would not disturb his parents or his friends "for so little". So, did my arrival have *so little* significance? His words made me quickly realize that even his neighbours were not aware of my presence! Therefore, the overwhelming joy that I had imagined, with a warm welcome accentuated by intense and very nice moments that George and I would share with people he loved, was unfortunately drowned in my partner's cold and authoritarian tone when he disconcertingly stressed, without looking at me, that my coming was nobody's business, except his. And while his massive grey tabby cat came running into the lounge to curl around his legs, he turned his face away from me, looking more sedate and delicate. He revealed to me that he had no friends in the neighbourhood, let alone in the building, because he did not share anything with his neighbours, apart from the common areas. Affectionately stroking the cat that was now in his arms, he added that this was how people lived here; with no doubt, I would eventually get used to it over time. His gentleness with the animal was really moving, thus prompting me to seek, if necessary, the same bond. And, reassured by my conciliatory character and the passion of his obvious love that gave me considerable pride, I internally decided that nothing, ever, could discourage me from this good-natured and irresistibly adorable man, who was offering me a very promising emotional life.

After dinner, driven on by common passion owing to our wonderful connection and George's extreme kindness, I entirely sank into his charming hands, becoming a party to his intimate gestures. We made love in a greedy way for a long moment, then by means of languorous caresses on my face he outlined the most beautiful stanzas of a short rhyme-free poem written for me, praising my big brown eyes covered by thick eyebrows, my well-aligned teeth and my fleshy lips, the mole printed on the corner of my left ear and my tightly curled short black hair that he liked to touch. Never had a man showed me so much thoughtfulness. So I lost myself in compliments from my partner who had taken a day off to enjoy our reunion, strengthened by our carnal embraces and our first confidences. Therefore, I was filled with an inner well-being that I had never felt with a man I trusted, George, because he assured me of his deep love, thus giving me the extreme satisfaction that I had found what many young girls in my country were still looking for: a sensitive and caring man capable of undivided attention which gives you the impression of being a princess. So I tried to register this fabulous moment in my memory to recount it in detail to my mother especially, while inwardly, I never ceased to thank God for this exceptional happiness. I felt special, different. As George was going to go back to work the following day, he promised to take me out to visit Paris, the Eiffel Tower and the Champs-Elysees over the forthcoming weekend. I was very happy and my fear of the unknown land disappeared completely.

IV

My first visit to George's parents was an introduction to my new life. The previous day, a very ambitious George got down to teaching me how to speak *French-French*; because his parents were not accustomed to my African-French accent, it would have been difficult to communicate with them. He presented me with the opportunity to improve my French speech as a beneficial chance for me before looking for a job. Trusting the merits of his initiative I soon forgot the embarrassment I first had at the thought that he was ashamed of my accent now that we were in France, because he made no comment about it during his visit to my country. Moreover, like most young people of my country, I liked white people's intonation that we imitated when watching their movies. Similarly, more than any other outward sign, when I went back home, my way of speaking would mark my access to Westernization. Instantly, I became a good student, willing to saying each of my sentences again after he had corrected them or, like a child learning their first words, repeating what I heard him say, even without his knowledge. And when he was not at home, I practised my French diction through the different TV shows I watched. In particular, Jean-Luc Reichmann became my language mentor because I loved his various imitations and mimicries of the candidates he hosted in his noon daily show that I never missed.

Two weeks after my arrival, his parents wanted to meet me. One Saturday morning, George and I first took a train to Paris and from there we got into another which brought us closer to the remote hamlet where his parents lived, at the entrance of a small town in the direction of Orleans. A few steps away from the station, strolling along a deserted sidewalk next to George, I was quite confused. And, sensing my concern as we proceeded, George spontaneously told me everyone had a car in the area: his father had offered to pick us up at the station, but he had refused to allow us to have a romantic breath of air through the village. I found his initiative so flattering that my heart was carried away again. Arm in arm, we shortly talked of our respective parents. Then all along the way, which lasted about fifteen minutes, we had a longer discussion about his work situation, especially because he had recently felt tired and thought he deserved some rest. He rejoiced in spending time with his family, away from his home where he could not resist the temptation to write on his computer. I felt that he was questioning the relevance of his employment status, because he did not earn as much money as he hoped. I was a little surprised to hear him talk about money so long, as he had never shown any peculiar attraction for material things. Instead, I appreciated his generosity towards me, so that the bitterness evident in his voice seemed a bit exaggerated. I then suggested he took time to think in order to put things into perspective, to which he replied that he had been hesitating for several days to make a choice that could do him good. By making that decision, he might offend others... but at least he would be doing something for him and him alone... because he should think about himself! I approved his resolution without prying into what he had in mind as I knew that whatever would make him happy would positively and ultimately affect me.

When we arrived at destination, Clarisse and Joseph, his parents, were waiting at the threshold to their house. Both looked at me with interest, and were friendly, thus passing on to me the joy that made this moment quite warm. Overtaking her husband on the doorstep, Clarisse and her impressive liveliness walked towards us and kissed me vigorously before hugging her son, while a more reserved Joseph waited until we got to him to hug us, one after the other. Clarisse was wearing a knee-length azure blue dress exhibiting the pencil traces that failed to conceal the black stitches that were evidence of a fresh and quick alteration. Her smile did not leave her mouth until her rough little hand, which was squeezing mine, showed me the way to their lounge that was separated from the main door by a rectangular picture window surrounding the superb porch decorated with flowerpots and plants whose names I did not know.

Once settled in, proving to be more talkative than her husband, Clarisse started whispering questions to George:

"We can understand everything she says... the little Miss?" She observed in a curious voice.

"Yes... they speak French in her country, you know." At the same time, he threw a quick glance at me, and then continued, "She is pretty, isn't she?"

Clarisse did not answer because she saw that I had heard him. She tried to hide her embarrassment by speaking directly to me.

"I have never visited Africa. Is your country big?"

"Yes, but not as big as France."

"It seems that you have good weather all the time..."

"True, but sometimes it is very cold... during the rainy season."

"But you have summer all the time..."

"We don't call it summer... we have no summers. We only have the rainy season and the dry season."

"Ah, it's so different from us!"

"Yes, quite different..."

Because I suddenly understood that Clarisse did not know Africa as much as I knew her country, with great pride I undertook to tell her a bit more about my culture, our eating habits, and above all, upon her persistence, the way we dressed during traditional ceremonies. She also wanted to know if our lifestyle was really different from what she had seen on television and she sometimes seemed to sympathize with our poverty in terms that troubled me, as her voice took a pitying tone that set me on the defensive. So I tried to paint a conceited picture of the Africa I knew, rich in foodstuffs, human warmth and full of resources that unfortunately we did not use. Since I did not wish to appear pessimistic at all, I explained that many young people would leave my country with the hope to return one day, better equipped to contribute to its development. My words proved unnecessary for Clarisse whose expression changed immediately. I realised that she did not like being thwarted. So I stopped my praise of Africa to hear her instead. Afterwards, Clarisse monopolized my attention for half an hour at least, getting me involved in a harmonious discussion that made me feel that a good camaraderie had developed between us. The enthusiasm her crystal clear and strong voice was spreading throughout the living room filled me with confidence, erasing the fear and distrust inspired by her imposing stout frame.

Meanwhile, her husband, who was busy informing his son of his latest farming works, served us an appetizer. With a distant look, Joseph handed me a glass of white wine, without saying a word, then gave his son and his wife a glass of red wine. With black sparkling eyes Clarisse was the first to raise her glass for a toast. Her wide smile made her very thin lips disappear completely, revealing a chaotic and mottled set of teeth. We copied her gesture. Then she wanted to continue our conversation, which we did until we were interrupted by George who reminded her that he never eats before visiting them, because he knew she will feed him with plentiful fresh food. Clarisse burst out laughing, and then got up immediately while teasing her son whom she took to the kitchen walking in a determined way, while I stayed in the parlour with Joseph.

Since we had entered their home, Joseph had had very little regard for me, as if he had nothing to say. His observant appearance gave the impression that he was extremely shy. However, I soon noticed the opposite when he proved to be unpleasant to me as I was trying to engage him in a conversation to get to know him. His hoarse voice suddenly sounded masterful and insensitive and deftly conveyed the whole cruel and unthinkable aversion he felt towards me. First of all, he accused me of having charmed his son to escape destitution... and, looking overwhelmed by disgust, he then pointed out the fact that his son was not responsible for Africa's poverty and should not pay the price for it! I had goose bumps all over my skin. Hearing such words from the mouth of this incredibly quiet man whose tender eyes darkened under the weight of his bushy eyebrows was shocking. I watched him for a long time, a bit frightened, to realize that as terrible as he looked, he fortunately had no ability to attack me physically because of his frail appearance despite his stocky body. George had effectively warned me of his health problems as well as his impulsiveness. So I decided to be smart by keeping a cool head in order to act in the most appropriate way in this rather delicate circumstance, and also to avoid infuriating him. He seemed surprised and literally paralysed; so much that discomfort spontaneously emerged on his wrinkled face. He withdrew into himself. He did not speak for the ten minutes we sat one in front of the other, in silence, with elusive eyes, until the return of George who came to tell us the meal was ready.

I had never tasted sausages in my life, and specifically the unbearable smell of cabbage and other ingredients that composed the meal. I almost lost my appetite. George said it was sauerkraut. I ate a little bit of it only to pay tribute to Clarisse's hard work, but I expressly concentrated on the ratatouille that reminded me of one of the vegetable stews my mother often cooked.

After the meal, I helped Clarisse in the kitchen. She praised my sweetness, my dedication and my kindness, though it was our very first meeting. She particularly enjoyed my mildness, which she compared to that of a modern woman who was nevertheless submissive and respectful of traditions. This finally made me believe that our habits were not as different as I had imagined. After long minutes of a monologue where my contributions were limited to monosyllabic answers, Clarisse told me she was happy that her son had finally found a young black woman worthy of him. I was delighted because I knew that her husband had a different point of view. But it was out of question to discuss Joseph's deceitful and totally unexpected coldness with anyone. Clarisse also confessed that the first time George had brought them a black fiancée, she, in particular, struggled to accept her because, as she said, "those people" were strange, but I looked fairly civilized. She also told me that George had finally got rid of this young woman a few months before the date set for their wedding because of her weird practices: she believed in ancestor worship and honoured the dead instead of celebrating All Saints' Day like everyone else. She added that George had informed her that I had always lived in town in my country, and therefore I learnt their way of living through movies.

Since our aborted conversation Joseph had been even less talkative, but his scornful eyes confirmed to me at that moment that he regarded me as a true savage coming straight from the bush. I hid my uneasiness as best as I could to avoid offending our hosts, and I turned myself towards George. But, until our departure, despite my disappointment, I decided not to tell George anything about his father's sour criticism as I did not want useless confrontation, unless he brought it up, if by any means he had noticed something or had Joseph himself mentioned his hostile feelings towards me. Besides, I owed as much to the short lady whose round and wrinkled face was written with unrivalled cheerfulness, because she had really tried to receive me decently contrarily to her husband and had opened her house and her heart to me like a mother. In fact, I felt obliged to compromise to avoid any controversy. Particularly, because the situation was quite tricky, and to avoid a serious conflict with my partner, I hastily determined to put my good will to the fore and persist in my decision to forget Joseph's sad allegations.

All the time we had known each other, George had never discussed his past love life with me, except for the fact that, as he used to say, he had suffered a lot from a previous relationship, which had made him become withdrawn for a long time and to look for a more docile African lady, because he particularly liked *Blacks*. For him, getting a girlfriend was not difficult at all, but a good wife was not easy to find, above all in his circle. He had observed that nobody, namely among his friends, was really happy with their white partner. He was pessimistic, or rather worried, but I was soon relieved to hear that with me he had finally found the wife he had been looking for: obliging, obedient, thoughtful and loving. I believed his words were sincere, because I had heard him telling people several times that he had brought his *black* fiancée from Africa. In the beginning, I prided myself on those occasions when he would allow me to speak to his friends on the phone when they wished to congratulate me on managing to win him over. But without knowing, they mainly wanted to assess my degree of civility, as I understood when George confirmed to one of them that I was not antisocial because my country was somewhat developed, anyway, much more than he had imagined before going there. I was upset to hear that my dear friend was introducing me that way. But it did not matter much as he continued to be very nice to me.

During the following months, for the very first time, he invited one of his friends home. The latter did not hide his curiosity as he was single. He wished to get in touch with a young lady who was as slender and brilliant as he said I was. I immediately took that as a godsend opportunity to make someone dear to me come to France as well, so I would no longer feel isolated. Thus, my first idea was to give him the contact details of my little sister, then aged nineteen. However, it finally occurred to me that it was too early to consider her trip, even if she was given this chance, when I was still not certain of my own situation. Besides, I was afraid that planning her trip would urge her to disregard her studies; and, if things did not work out positively for her, I would have been responsible for her disarray. Doubtful, I decided to direct the determined suitor towards one of my best friends, Colette, who was also looking for a white.

I had been sharing George's life for about two months, and the way he treated me filled me with euphoric joy. One evening, after his return from work, I asked him permission to call my parents as they had not heard from me since the day of my arrival. Always very compassionate, George told me that he had been thinking of suggesting that to me.

On the phone, George was the first to talk to my mother and he expressed his deep gratitude and joy. My mother also said she was happy for us and blessed us, wishing our union to be peaceful and very fruitful. I told her that my new life was an extraordinary experience and my well-being unrivalled, which did not lead me to regret leaving my friend Colette or my other mates to whom I had promised to write as often as possible. In fact, I had the feeling of being venerated by a handsome prince who recited poems to me after moments of intense intimacy. Yes, George was in love with me. Clarisse loved me and actually behaved like a mother to me, and even if I did not understand much about Joseph's unfriendliness, my mother and I were beside ourselves with joy. We both wept, and then said a prayer of thanksgiving before hanging up.

However, the first quarter went much too fast. George was working as a special education advisor and he was responsible for working with young people doomed to educational failure. His role was primarily to help prevent young people unsuited to the educational system to gain independence and the confidence they needed to be able to integrate socially and professionally. His timetable was very flexible as his activities, which I sometimes found funny, led him to travel the Parisian region with some of the students he was in charge of, to meet other people or visit cultural places such as museums and theatres. As a result, he sometimes got up very early at five o'clock in the morning. I liked to spend as much time as possible with him, so every morning to keep him company, I got up at the same time as him to prepare his breakfast while he was getting ready. Other times, he worked until late, so we had time to talk a bit in the morning. He found his work fascinating because he was sure he was contributing to the social development of his students, some of whom avoided erratic behaviour and distractions thanks to him. George also admitted that his job required him to use lots of energy, which made him sometimes very irascible when he returned home. I reassured him that he was strong and his open-mindedness helped him to face reality as much as it enabled him to always be a good advisor. Similarly, his vigour and lifestyle that he seemed to be proud of gave him maturity, a touching delicacy and availability for whomever was his ally. That was how I understood his desire for quietude on the days he did not work or when he spent many hours in front of his computer screen to escape into writing and rewriting of poems he always refused to let me read.

As for me, my day was reduced to sleeping, waking up, watching television, cooking meals or cleaning the house while waiting for George's return. He had made it clear that he did not want me to use the phone in his absence, so I ended up thinking that the way I talked and my accent were still not adequate. I always respected this rule, hoping for a change soon. Sometimes, when he was late and the sun was heating the walls of the apartment excessively, I would sit by the window to get some fresh air while watching the passersby and vehicles. However, once he was back, very often I had to repress my desire to speak, and silently appreciated his efforts to make me feel at ease so that I never lacked anything. And, when he was around and not feeling too tired, he would take me for a stroll around the neighbourhood. Unfortunately, these trips never lasted long enough and we had to go back because he was rather homely and always had something to do on the Internet or telephone.

Until then, I had never experienced such a thing in my country, where all doors are mostly wide open from morning to sunset when we closed them, primarily to prevent inadvertent entry of mosquitoes or flies. Even in remote villages, for fear of being surprised by wild animals that could accidentally be seen along the path leading to our farms, house keys were always hidden under a front porch, the location of which was known by every neighbour. Therefore, I felt a bit claustrophobic. Furthermore, despite George's punctuality, I was very lonely. More than once, I tried to explain my growing unease to my partner, but he listened with one ear, pretending that I would eventually get used to it. However, over time, this loneliness began racing out of control and gradually broke up my happiness. The ambivalence of my state of mind, because I was still happy, made me very confused. These past three months doing nothing, moving around inside four cold walls, began to affect my daily life. And George saw nothing! The joy that used to emerge from our relationship was now replaced by an overwhelming monotony. Once again, George told me that this was the way people lived in France and, with time, I would find my bearings.

V

I was about to spend my first Christmas in France. One afternoon, Clarisse phoned. Her son was not home yet, but I recognized her voice on the answering machine. I rushed to pick up the phone. I had not heard from her since the end of the summer, apart from regular greetings sent to me through George. The few times we had talked in the past, she had always displayed good humour, but this time I found her particularly reserved and cautious, as if surprised to find me at home. She stammered irresolute words; she wanted to invite us during the festive season for a family get-together. Her coldness was catching, and imitating the austerity of her tone, I replied that I would pass the message on to her son. What else could I say? The many silences accumulated in our conversation rushed onward to a relieving goodbye on both sides. Not knowing what to think of the attitude of this extravagant woman who, until now, had shown great kindness. I was determined to have a word with her son later.

George came home at the same time as usual. On his way, he had bought supplies for the kitchen, cleaning and for the cat's litter. He gave me the bags of provisions upon entering the apartment. I went into the kitchen and placed them on the ground. I returned to the main room.

"Your mother phoned this morning," I simply said to George.

"Let me hear the message," he replied.

"I answered, and she seemed surprised to find me here..."

"You answered?" He stammered, as if I had just announced a disaster.

"She wants us to spend Christmas as a family, but she sounded reserved and cold with me."

"Perhaps because she didn't expect you to answer *my* phone!"

"But when I heard her voice, I thought I could pick it up," I murmured shyly.

George flew into a terrible rage. He was beside himself, and shouted, almost threatening me, "What possessed you to touch my phone? Who do you think you are? Haven't I warned you that... ah, that's how you thank me for helping you out of misery? Without *me* where would you be right now? You'd be nothing... you'd be selling doughnuts on the run in your village... but it's not enough for you to be here! And you want to do the opposite of what I'm saying? Want to decide for me, now?"

While George was still fuming, cursing me with his eyes blazing with anger and his furious gestures, I was prostrated on the sofa, both overwhelmed by his reaction and horrified by the unexpected violence of his words.

I was shocked by the sudden and excessive discontent which, in fact, showed his latent hostility and exasperation, to the extent that I could not speak for a long time. I also waited until I was calmer internally to talk to him.

"George!" I called him, as always in a deferential tone.
He gave me that look that can make you dumb. But the horrific scene he had just showed me quickly defeated my fear.
"Why do you treat me like that?"
"How do I treat you?" He replied dryly.
"Why are you talking to me like that?" I said quietly hoping to alleviate my friend's irritation. Then I continued, "Is it only because of the phone or is there anything else behind all this?"
"You really want to know?" he said, stressing his response with large protruding eyes followed by a sarcastic laugh.

Now, I feared what would come out of his mouth. He started speaking again. I almost jumped at the sound of his voice, because I did not recognize the one that had seduced me. It was terrifying. My heart was pounding.

"You know how much you've cost me since I met you? Among other things, the money I sent you when you were there in your village... all the money I spent on your trip, and I have to go out every day to feed you... you know how much you're costing me? It's all my savings, yes, all my savings, just for you... and you are unable to do what I tell you to do?"

His hurtful words struck my head like a violent shock that pierced my chest. I remained motionless for a moment, almost inert. Then, I sat up on the couch with my eyes set on his. I was ready to listen to everything he had to say in his clearly regrettable and liberating anger. Equally, his serious eyes kept staring at me to ensure that I had understood him properly. Despite being gravely bewildered, I nodded, not to approve his reaction, but to make him understand that he had actually exposed an unexpected and hidden part of him, and then I lowered my eyes. I kept my head bowed as long as his impulsive and reproachful monologue lasted and only raised it once he left the living room all the while muttering.

"So there we are... my friends warned me! All these Africans, all the same... nothing but plunderers... you'll never touch my money... ever... I know you only look forward to obtaining your papers to get your claws out, Tigress. But you're wrong. Stop dreaming... Remember that your visa has expired for some time, I can send you back to your village whenever I want..." he yelled, "do you hear me? When I want!... and instead of considering herself happy with my forbearance, she wants to annoy me...."

The protective love that was blinding me had just seen its veil torn away by his belittling remarks and by the disparaging statements which revealed the depths of his mind. For long minutes, George's unambiguous words had the effect of a terribly offensive eye-opener, which then made me realize that since my arrival, I still knew nothing about our neighbourhood because George did everything alone. He gave me everything I needed, but cleverly locked me up in his apartment, never letting me out without him, only to visit his parents, go shopping or browse around the vicinity. Visiting the Eiffel Tower and the Champs-Elysees had never happened. So, his friends have advised him to be careful because I would let him down once I got my residence permit thanks to him. I was totally dazed.

The silence that followed this incident was so awkward and confusing that only the walls had a lively appearance in the apartment. The dividing walls were vibrating from the refrigerator's humming in the kitchen while, above my head, footstep squeaks were echoing on the floor. In the bedroom where George had locked himself in with his cat, no noise. Overwhelmed by a sudden unruly languor, I remained in a prostrate position for over an hour.

Usually, when I was attacked in this manner, I immediately dissolved into tears, because being of a rather peaceful nature, I knew how to avoid confrontation in order not to inflame an already tense situation. Worst of all, even if I wanted to respond, the fear of being thrown out sealed my mouth. Instead, I asked myself questions. What was happening? Within minutes, George had just emptied all his contempt for me and my culture. I could hardly believe what my ears had heard. But I resolved to ask for an explanation once calmness had resumed, since his anger seemed highly disproportionate. Because of his unfailing kindness since our first physical contact, I wanted to believe that this fury was not directly addressed to me. After a while, George calmed himself down and moved over to his computer where he continued muttering complaints intermittently. Listening with one ear, I carefully overheard him and I soon realized he was actually complaining about my presence in his house. This filled me with sorrow because I knew my status in his apartment had now changed. "What a misfortune," I thought to myself. Time for indulgence had really expired. I had to take due note of it! However, far from being prepared for this new situation, I wanted to rebel, at least to tell him my mind, but silence was necessary because his sidestepping of dialogue forbade any explanation. In addition, I knew I had no other option before me: where was I going to go if I was forced to leave his home?

Similarly, in my mind Clarisse's coldness reappeared. I guessed at the muddy gossip she and her son had bathed me in to debase me, without giving me the opportunity to defend myself, so that, for her, I was a contagious fiend whose negative emanation could defile her. Mother and son, accomplices united in a whirlwind of lies, I incessantly repeated to myself, with a heavy heart, to console myself for my own lack of courage to verbalize my thoughts to him. My blood was boiling with humiliation and resentment against George to whom my eyes turned slowly.

For the first time that evening, I noticed huge discreet wrinkles behind his glasses that hid his misty eyes. His slightly crooked nose had erased affability from his face, and one or two grey hairs stood out in his small goatee even though he regularly tinted it to hide his age. As usual, after work, he was wearing one of his pairs of jeans he liked so much as they made him feel younger and helped him conceal our seventeen-year age difference. More than ever, he looked squeezed into this garment because of his short legs. He seemed to have shrunk further, which gave him a thug-like appearance. I intently watched him for about ten minutes as his back was facing me. I wondered what might have given him the assurance of becoming so narcissistic to prompt him to always seek his reflection to admire his face and repeat "What a handsome man!" These words had never bothered me before, but now their echo in my head infuriated me: how could such a man adore himself and praise his success with women? He had known so many that he was unable to name them all. Many questions sprang into my head. Why then did he hunt for a pen-girlfriend thousands miles away from his home if he was as confident and as attractive as he claimed to be, if his sex appeal was so unfailing? I was too preoccupied with the new equation that had established itself in my life to try to understand my friend's unpredicted attitude. Confusion was added to my calculations because, obviously, I had no choice but to bear his whims, as upsetting as they were.

From then on, whatever George said sounded false. I was concerned: how would I be able to get out of this foreign country without a residence permit, without any desire to live with such an arrogant man who had just voiced all his disrespect for me? There, back home, everyone was convinced that suffering was inexistent in France, either physical or emotional. How many times had I gathered with my friends to criticize our men whom we often compared to whites… so sensitive and loving people! No one would understand my complaints, especially after complimenting him for so many months. Although my confidence was definitely shaken, it was out of the question to run away. So, I resolved to stay with George, at least to get my residence permit, and then I would move on. In fact, the way I viewed George changed slowly but surely. In him I saw no more than a self-centred partner who was not very concerned about my future. Consequently, I had no more reason to worry about his apprehensions, just mine.

Several days passed. Things returned to normal. I finally realized that no discussion was possible with my boyfriend. Hence, I felt it necessary to find a way out all by myself. So every day, once he had left home, I searched through my old notebook and called the few numbers that were in there. At first it was not obvious, since I was just trying to reconnect with people I was not related to, just to find a listening ear that would be nearer in terms of distance if not in feelings, like my mother. Some people I talked to were very pleasant and answered me favourably, but were unwilling to satisfy my implicit request for ongoing closeness. Besides, not having George's permission to receive phone calls, I could not give anyone our number, so, when we said goodbye, I promised to call them occasionally, knowing I would never do it again.

With the likelihood of establishing new friendships quickly aborted, George's wrath, which sounded like a dramatic scene, was sadly replayed in my mind when I felt misunderstood, urging me to inform my family whenever he was not home. One morning, I told my mother the most recent events. As expected she advised me to be patient because there were ups and downs for every couple, and as much as she knew George, she found excuses for his latest fury. She revived my feelings, saying I was exaggerating things because I had surely misinterpreted his fit of anger. At that moment, I sensed that there was nothing I could do, given my parents' tremendous consideration for him, especially as joie de vivre had established itself in their home since I left and its expression was made by my mother's inexhaustible thanks that she repeatedly addressed to God for the magnificent destiny He had reserved for her child.

During the following month, George and I were closer again. An excellent harmony united us. One evening, as we sat at his desk and discussed past conflicts as I had hoped, both of us were surprised at the ease with which we were able to forgive each other. I considered it to be another sign of destiny, since George was as supportive as he used to be before, nevertheless he no longer recited poems to me. But also, he bought me flowers once for no particular reason. It was Friday and he was on his way back from work. This was the only time because this gesture was never renewed. It did not matter much compared to the maintenance of peace that I considered to be essential for my fulfilment. So I had to learn to live with his mood swings.

We spent a happy Christmas with his family. As I looked at all the guests Clarisse had invited, I quickly realized that I was the only black person around. Once again, after the first moments of general kindness, my presence aroused a lot of curious and intrusive questions about my family, but mostly there were whispers that served as the appetizer. I retreated into silence because George was consistently showing himself to be dominant towards me, I just wanted to become invisible. I understood that his aim was to prove to the audience that he had managed to tame me. Despite the reminders of his mother whose hypocrisy was tinged with a touch of frustrating compassion, he remained very condescending, wanting me to obey his orders without batting an eyelid. I played the game, remaining strong and hoping that his spirit would come out of the darkness that had invaded him since our dispute: the submissive woman obeying her spouse! I had no choice. The fear within me since I realized that George could have me expelled from France at any moment forced me to endure all the humiliations he would expose me to, as they could not last forever.

When back home, a few days after the New Year, one morning as he was not busy with housekeeping, George went out for a few hours. He had stopped taking me along to visit the neighbourhood or stroll around for a long time. Still, to maintain our peacefulness, I never moaned, in spite of my numbing routine, which went by second by second, with no other distraction but cooking, television and the window from which I regularly watched passersby and vehicles, and, on the horizon, the ballet of dancing tree leaves in the afternoon's breeze. Sometimes, for a change, I would flip through one of those women's magazines he bought me from time to time to allow myself to follow fashion styles, learn how to keep our humble apartment trendy or learn to cook the French cuisine with ingredients the names of which I did not know. The first time he offered me a magazine to that end, I really thought his suggestion was dire mockery, given the old furniture and the limited means available to live on. Over time, this habit of my partner showed me just that he aspired to a life he could not afford. It also made me think that he had brought me from Africa to raise his own status and to prove something to his family and friends, not because he loved me.

When George came back, loaded with a big bag and four jumpers he had bought for himself, he begun justifying himself: he had a credit note in a shop so he had gone to get the jumpers to settle it. I had not asked him for anything. So, I concluded that he might have felt bad about buying himself something when he could not give me a gift. It did not matter at all. Having grown up in a poor family where our life was organized according to my father's daily revenue alone, we could afford only the most important things, admittedly by compromising or through deprivation sometimes, but at least without begging. We did not expect anything from anyone before George entered our family with the promises involved. Instead, to wear the latest fashions, I used to content myself with the idea of going to the flea market with my friends, early in the morning to welcome new deliveries. Indeed we made sure we were the first to delve into the batches coming from Europe, in search of designer clothes that had not been worn a lot. So, George did not have to bother for me. I did not show any emotion. However, the more I refused to give in to his vexatious actions, the more my emotional stability was weakening and my resentment amplifying. At the same time, I was sure to fully control the situation... and I therefore thought it fit to appear in a new way, using silence as a means of pressure which proved to be effective: George finally tried to find a way to compensate for his indelicacy by undertaking to take me to visit the icy streets of Paris on the following Saturday.

That day was full of wonders. We were both very happy to walk together on the noisy sidewalks of the Champs-Elysees, which was my childhood dream. My eyes were illuminated by the cleanliness of the streets; wanderers were strolling relaxing on both sides of the road lined with huge richly decorated windows that we occasionally admired. After an hour we found ourselves at the other end of the fabulous avenue, where a large roundabout was opening on several streets. I asked George to walk down the street towards the Eiffel Tower, as we could see its top from where we were. We took a bus that dropped us less than a mile from the monument. For the first time, at last, I had the sensation of being in another world and my change of scene was complete: Paris was alive! We crossed the bridge, hand in hand. I was the only one to talk, because I had so many memories of films I wanted to quickly tell my partner before getting to the Tower's huge metal legs. A large number of tourists was waiting to climb its staircases to explore it from inside. I dropped George's hand to get close to one leg of the Tower that I repeatedly stroked. My heart quivered with joy. For a brief moment I was transported: since my arrival, I was withdrawn in a life that would have been unthinkable if I had been living back home, and this could not continue. Over there, life existed outside and having my friends around gave it a delicious savour, mainly when we strolled about or hung around young men whose main daily work was to play the *ludo*, the *songo* or cards for money, while downing litres of beer purchased by one or the other. Why should I undergo this captive treatment? Me? So proud and haughty to young men in my neighbourhood. How could I have become so dependent? Some of them would have been shocked to know what I was going through. I did not even recognize myself in this passive woman, which made me think I was lucky not to know anyone in Paris, because it spared me the shameful gossips. In my country, nobody was aware of how I lived in France, with George. It was better that way. Yet, many questions flashed through my head. I was frightened. Was I afraid of novelty or of deceiving myself? Why all this? Because I was in a foreign country... because my visa was no longer valid and because I had to restrain myself until George helped me to get a residence permit?

Once back in our little suburban apartment, I thanked George for his pleasant surprise. He was also delighted but soon sounded regretful when he sourly told me that I should not expect this to happen often because it was costly. He had to spend carefully since he had two mouths to feed; and the way things were going he would soon not be able to cope. I took advantage of his statement to suggest the idea of finding a job, housekeeping or even babysitting around our area. He adamantly opposed that because he did not want me to enter any house in our vicinity. Then I stated that if I could get my residence permit, I could work to increase our household income. To this idea he seemed more favourable. He also added that he had been thinking of something like that for some time because it was not normal to stay at home without doing anything for almost a year. His aim, by shutting me away, was actually to ensure I had enough confidence to travel around all alone and to contribute to our household needs. Even if that seemed to be contradictory, I could not help rejoicing. George was very unpredictable. I thought that time and patience would enable me to know him better, and like my mother said, "things would fall into place by themselves again". Anyway, the idea of working, getting out of this apartment and meeting other people would be so fulfilling that I looked forward to it and wanted to know when, where and how we were going to proceed. Despite all, a slight anxiety remained in me owing to his sudden mood swings. Accordingly, I stifled my excitement by adopting a laid-back attitude. Besides, having received a message from Colette, through my mother who informed me that her correspondence with George's friend had ended because the young man had asked her to find a way to travel to France by her own means since he distrusted those African women asking men for money, I felt blessed to have met George. My mother also told me that my friend had insisted on my exceptional fortune in finding one of the rare, generous white men who were still available in Europe and as such it was in my interest to concede everything to him and, of course, to always remember that. Her words were of great comfort to me. I lifted my eyes upwards to thank Heaven once again, because Colette's misfortune really made me believe in my lucky star.

A few weeks later, George came back from work incredibly cheerful.

"Yvette, I have some good news for you," he said, as he opened the door.

I was in the kitchen. I came out immediately to kiss him as usual.

"I have had a conversation about you... with a friend of mine."

"Well!"

"Yeah. I often told him you'd like to work and..."

"Oh, that's great..."

"Wait a minute... his wife and him are running a small business that is successful. They help young African girls like you when they want to work... even if they have no working permits."

That information made me understand that George was acquainted with some African circle, even if he did not openly admit it. I was more reassured by that, as such proximity could help him understand my problems and especially my instinct of solidarity for my family. My concern was mainly for my brothers who had dropped out of school, were jobless and wandering throughout the day in our neighbourhood, without any hope of seeing them finding a solution to inactivity, as nobody in our family was related to the elitist civil servants who could pull strings for them within an administrative office.

One evening, George came back from work along with his friend, Jude. What a handsome man! Elegantly dressed in a grey tailored suit, he entered our apartment, walking gracefully. His long, square face displayed a smile that showed off his childish looks. When he saw me, he congratulated George for his good taste because he found me to his liking and joked that if George did not want me anymore, he should consider calling him. While I was active getting the dinner ready, Jude and George were discussing various things. However, my interest was aroused when I overheard them talk about the possibility of me working with someone named Jesabel. I then pricked up my ears to hear well. Thus I caught bits and pieces of their conversation: my tall size and my measurements suited him, and especially the delicate features of my fair face gave the impression that I was mixed. Afterwards, they lingered on that other individual, Jesabel, who was the key person because she would have the final word anyway.

Once the meal was ready, we all ate together. They continued their conversation while I remained passive but attentive to George's actions as usual. Eventually, the two men informed me that I was going to meet Jesabel, Jude's wife, who was going to show me the way to get a job because, as I understood, she had been in the business for three or four years. Neither of them told me what the job was all about. I was motivated and optimistic as I thought things were going just the way I wanted, even more so as the situation reminded me of my country where it was necessary to know someone in an office to be able to get a good job. The refined aspect of this individual, who looked forty or so and who undoubtedly took great care of his physical appearance, redoubled my enthusiasm. Therefore, no matter the task I was going to be assigned to, I knew I would be able to fulfil it, even if I had not attended school beyond the baccalaureate, because my parents did not have enough money to pay the university fees and for the endless lists of books. At the time, my father thought it was pointless spending money on my studies, as brilliant as I was, because such an investment would not have guaranteed me a good job anyway. So, he employed me partially in his shop, without salary, just to spare me from the chronic inactivity that struck most helpless young graduates. Therefore when I was not at the shop, I often spent my afternoons with my idle friends, wasting our time without ambition, expecting to meet with a responsible husband who would take us out of our daily monotony.

About two weeks after Jude's visit, Clarisse phoned and, amazingly, George allowed me to talk to her. She did not beat about the bush to advise me to always remember to be grateful to her son who had found a job for which she heartily congratulated me. I was incapable of answering her with anything else but a hesitant "thanks". Immediately after that, I asked George how his mother knew about my situation before me; I thought nothing had been decided yet and I still had not heard from Jude and Jesabel. At that time, George informed me that Jesabel was not in Paris but at one of her provincial sites. He remained vague once again, but was explicit about the fact that Jude was awaiting her return any time soon. He would hasten our meeting once she was back. An immense joy seized my heart because I thought Jesabel must be a great lady, given her frequent trips and her husband's appearance and gait. I was really looking forward to getting to know her.

Since George had undertaken steps to find me a job, our relationship was stronger, more harmonious and unequivocal. A rainy night when he returned early, he told me he expected a lot from me. He hoped that I would work hard to enable us to significantly increase our income and promised that if everything worked out as planned, before spending three years in France, we could visit my family together. Hearing such a thing cast me into a reverie that I did not dare express: returning home, with my white husband, with suitcases full of gifts and money to distribute to my people? It was exactly what I was looking for. George was good at reading my mind. He always knew how to surprise me and managed to redeem his oversights. So I accepted his ongoing undertaking and definitely decided to work relentlessly when I started the job. It was all for our happiness, our well-being and above all for my own family's social achievement. I also promised George not to disappoint him.

One evening, my partner told me that he would drop me at Jesabel's the next morning before going to work. I had been waiting for this moment for weeks. I was apprehensive, fearing a different outcome to my expectations, so I preferred to keep quiet so as not to press George who had the capacity to destroy my hope. Now that the appointment was made, I became impatient. I wished to know how things would go since I still had no work permit. Without details, George said Jesabel would take care of everything and would answer all my questions; I should not be troubled, everything would be alright.

VI

George left me at Jesabel and Jude's apartment on his way to work. It was the beginning of the afternoon. As he did not know when we would be finished, he wrote instructions on a paper to help me go back home by train and gave me money for that purpose. He probably had high hopes of my interview to break two of his own rules this way, leaving me with other people and letting me travel across Paris, without a guide, for the very first time. Joy and excitement chased away my apprehension of that meeting. Soon, I figured out that once I was done with Jesabel a little impromptu stroll before returning home would do me a lot of good. And, comforted by the idea that she was an African like me, I thought of the friendship and trust we could build, which would reward me with an opportunity of another outing in Paris, owing to George's trust in her. But my partner stared at me intensely. I had the feeling that he had heard the exaltation of my awakened senses. His piercing eyes acted as a deterrent to my undisclosed project. I answered him, hesitating, that I could manage and make sure to go home as soon as I leave Jesabel's flat.

Jude opened the main door of a splendid apartment. His manly voice that had made him sound tough the first time we had met now sounded moderate when he introduced me to his wife, who was leaning on a chest, one hand on her hip, at the far end of the corridor facing the doorway. I moved towards her nervously. She stood up straight. Even more elegant than her husband, her chocolate and flawless complexion required no make-up to embellish the fine features of her angelic face. She was wearing a short plum dress that was so tight that it drew attention to her curves that were enhanced by high heels as well as her small size. Around her long neck hung a gold pendant engraved with the letters 'JC' and, on her right wrist, an English gold mesh bracelet. I did not have the courage to look at her. She was impressive. I was almost motionless for a moment before taking a seat on the beige leather sofa in front of her. I turned my eyes away from her dress to admire her fabulous lounge, which was decorated with modern furniture and wooden ornaments installed in a perfectly maintained glass display cabinet. My hostess was visibly very upset by a problem she was trying to settle over the telephone. She barely looked at me, only through furtive glances, without really worrying about my presence in the room. From time to time, her expression was stressed by extravagant and disturbing rigidity that took me aback. In the meantime, Jude served me fruit juice. Then he sat on the two-seater settee in front of me, but close enough to Jesabel who seemed not to notice him either. He was looking intimidated and waiting for her to end her conversation.

When she finally put the phone down, more than fifteen minutes later, a smile emerged on her bright red lips in my direction, unveiling perfect teeth. She asked her husband to leave us, which he did deferentially. Then she examined me from head to toe as she came to sit on the chair placed on my right. She immediately began a reassuring preliminary investigation of my background.

"So, how old are you?" she asked in a thin and singing voice.

"Twenty-seven."

"What are you doing here?" she said afterwards with indifference, which immediately drove away the sweetness I thought I had appreciated earlier.

"Um…" I murmured, feeling a bit lost and looking all around because I was destabilized by Jesabel's piercing gaze.

She went on without giving me time to respond, "Do you have friends?"

"Um…" I murmured again. "Here?"

"Where is your family?"

"Back home…"

"So, what can I do for you?" she asked, while her hand was rummaging through her handbag, out of which she brought her mobile phone.

"I thought that…"

"Wait!" she exclaimed in an imperative tone.

Jesabel dialled a number on her phone, and then set it to her ear. She hung up immediately, and later continued austerely, "What did you think?"

"But… uh… George told me that… uh… it's for the job…"

"What were you doing in your country?" she asked.

"I was working in my father's shop."

"Is that all?"

I was so surprised by her question that I did not know how to answer. So Jesabel spoke again. "Ha… ha… ha… your father's shop could enable you come to France!" She laughed loudly while her face showed her sarcastic admiration.

Because of my persistent silence, she got impatient. "But… can't you speak? How did you travel here?"

"George helped me."

"I see… *I see.*"

Jesabel now wanted to know if I had been able to get a visa easily. I replied that I considered I was lucky to have been able to obtain it so quickly, after about a month. I also told her that for nearly a month I presented myself before the closed gate of the French Consulate every day, between three or four o'clock in the morning, wrapped in a big blanket because of the cool night. Each time, the same manoeuvre: a hundred people had preceded me and were already elbowing their way to gain a suitable place, desperate to enter the consulate when it opened some four to five hours later. Even so, of all the visa applicants hoping for a new start in life, only a few could get into the premises, unless strings had been pulled for them through the payment of a high price enabling their passing of the security guards. Thus, some of those officers increased their monthly pay by such illegal bargaining with complete impunity. Even so, there was no guarantee of obtaining the required visa once within the consulate. After several vain attempts, I also submitted to this means to get into the embassy and, fortunately, my application was crowned with success thanks to George's support.

Of course, Jesabel knew all that, so she interrupted me by subtly asking if I had had breakfast. I noticed a slight English accent in her intonation of certain words. As I replied positively she simply suggested increasing my drink. She got up, poured the juice into my half-emptied glass and then served herself too. As she was giving me the glass, I caught sight of a monstrous scar of a deep burn along her forearm. Jesabel read horror in my eyes and immediately said that she was used to this kind of reaction; I should not feel embarrassed because she was not bothered by the scar, which was just a legacy of her past. With compassion in my voice, I asked her if she had been burned by something as a child. She replied with an ironic laugh. It was the first time since we had been together that I saw her loosening her jaws like that. She laughed a minute, all alone, leaving me rather puzzled. Then, almost humming, she told me that this mark was her first husband's unalterable souvenir. I put the glass that I still held down on the table, looking inquisitive, browsing her arm and face in turn. She grabbed the question I did not dare to formulate and she began to explain everything.

She arrived in France in the late 1990s. Her parents were divorced, but agreed to buy her a plane ticket to go and 'manage on her own' in Europe to help her family after her elder sister died of AIDS, leaving two fatherless children. At her Sunday meeting, her mother met a woman whose daughter had lived in France for about three years. Whenever they met, this woman boasted about her thriving young girl who sent them money with astonishing regularity. And this had enabled her son to buy a car that was turned into a taxi, allowing the family to eat properly with the money he made every day. She and her husband had undertaken the building of a house in their village for their retirement. The lady's exhibited prosperity was spreading around all the women's mouths during their gatherings. So Jesabel's mother had strove to get money to send her daughter to France too, with her father's consent. At that time, Jesabel was working as a cashier in a grocer's in Lagos. She was thirty-two then and in a relationship with a policeman whom her parents disdained, because they suspected him of having other mistresses, so they dreaded the worst for their daughter. The final and compelling decision of the family council was not a thing to refuse, for fear of being rejected by all. Her mother had clearly advised her to be a 'go-getter', to work very hard in order to become 'someone' and not to return home penniless. In other words, her mission was to work for her family's social development by enabling them to improve their miserable living conditions, because the future of her brothers and sisters, as well as her nephews, was from then on in her hands. Thus prepared, Jesabel travelled to France where she met some fellow citizens and among them, the daughter of her mother's friend who was, as agreed, supposed to help her settle in.

During the first two weeks, she stayed with her compatriot. When the third week began, her housemate asked her to quickly find a man she could marry in order to get her residence permit because she would not be able to keep her any longer. In France, everyone had to look after themselves and not count on others. The young lady's cold reception was such that she was not in the position to stay at her apartment beyond three months. However, time went by quickly and she had already been around for two months. No job and no prospects for further developments in her life in this new environment. But she had been able to travel around the city alone and take steps. She had even tried to file for refugee status, which failed because her file lacked evidence of persecution in her homeland. Yet, those who had helped her file for asylum had told her it would be successful and therefore she would possibly receive support from social services during the investigation, which could take two years. Thus, it would have allowed her enough time to find somewhere to live and, maybe, start studying while doing moonlighting jobs, as a babysitter or as a cleaner. That first door being shut, and the three months approaching, her new acquaintances had organized a date with one of their compatriots who had been in France for about ten years and was looking for a soul mate. In the beginning, everything worked smoothly between her and the young man, who very quickly became her partner, and above all offered her the nest that welcomed her when she had no more accommodation.

She shared good feelings with her partner, until, although far away, the pressure of their families got the better of their relationship. On the one hand, her partner's family did not want her because she was from a poor family and marrying such a woman would add to their socio-economic problems; on the other hand, Jesabel's parents distinctly told her that she had not been sent to France to hunt for an African, because there were as many as she wanted back home! After about nine months of never-ending struggles to save their relationship, an ill-timed miscarriage occasioned numerous unconstructive comments from Jesabel's family about her partner, dealing the couple's relationship the last blow. She unenthusiastically left the man she loved and moved to Bordeaux, as an illegal citizen in the house of one of her friends who agreed to house her until her physical and emotional recovery. As she felt unable to adapt to the unkind treatment she started experiencing again because she had no home, after four months, she shortened her stay at her friend's by accepting the offer of a white man she had been seeing for a short time and who lived not far from the city centre. The man was single and suggested to her that she come under his roof after she had told him about her setbacks since her arrival in France. She then actually moved in with the man who became her boyfriend and promised to marry her quickly if she appeared docile and co-operative. The apprehension of returning home empty-handed, the teasing and mocking remarks she would endure and her family's sacrifice dictated that she should act selflessly.

Then began her torment with this man whose sexual appetite was insatiable and accompanied by violent embraces. She began to wonder if he was normal. Every day, she yielded to his whims, totally submitted. Sometimes she was forced to make love in an awkward position with her feet and her hands tied up, while her fiancé would use all kinds of items, just for fun. Her only moments of respite were when he was away at work. Jesabel took advantage of this time to meet other women with whom she talked, but never confided what she was going through, especially because her partner's atrocities were subtle and hardly noticeable. Many times, she tried to reveal her infamous secret, but terrified, she had resolved to remain silent, especially now that marriage was no longer relevant and had been replaced by blackmail of expulsion. She did not know where to go this time, so, she endured his abuse until the day her partner's violence was transformed into depravity as he was now using a whip: when they made love, he liked to hear her screaming and sobbing; but, as his usual practices did no longer hurt her as much as he wished, he had bought the whip and forced her to lie on her stomach to accomplish his perverted task.

One day, because she resisted, he lit a candle and burnt her forearm with the wax and the blazing flame. Despite her cries and tears, he only stopped when a worried neighbour knocked at their door. But her partner had shamelessly dismissed the individual and shut the door up. Later, seeing Jesabel's arm oozing more and more, he had undertaken to cool it in cold water for a few minutes with great indifference that was confirmed shortly after, when he went to hide in their bedroom after slamming the door behind him. Meantime, a distraught Jesabel had continued groaning in pain until sleep relieved her for a few hours. The following day, when she saw him leaving the house, she also rushed towards the train station, in the direction of Paris.

Jesabel told me her story without emotion, as if she had forgotten this rather painful episode of her life. The first impression I had of her, as a strong lady, was confirmed. I was so happy to have found someone like her who could understand me, because she had known poverty before the success she proudly displayed in her beautiful home. The phone rang. She responded and told me with her index finger to give her a minute. I felt a surge of compassion for her because of the abuse she had suffered and thought that for my greatest happiness, if she accepted my friendship as I sincerely hoped, I would rely on her experience and expertise to avoid the pitfalls of life in the Western world. Her story, like many others that I had heard when I used to live in my country, filled me with consideration for her, though her strength of character forbade me to externalize it. Now, I could not take my eyes off her: she was so beautiful and her presence and her bicolour hair extensions fascinated me. Clearly, this event had strengthened her more and I thought that behind her deliberate arrogance laid a charitable heart. So I longed to hear what she had to offer to help me gain my financial independence and I had no doubt that she would lend me a hand to accomplish the mission my family had entrusted me with.

Once available, Jesabel now took a little time to ask me questions, especially about my skills. I answered as she continued to converse with another person on the phone. But I noticed surprisingly that it did not prevent her from listening to me. She seemed quick-tempered tough, and realistic at the same time, and felt there was no shame in blackmail, because I heard her threatening her interlocutor repeatedly. And when she spoke to me, intermittently, her contempt for others became apparent as much as the gossip flowing from her mouth described her pitiful personality. I suddenly wondered how such a pretty strong, intelligent and straightforward character who also inspired fear could behave so pathetically. Her behaviour showed me that she was emotionally inclined to harm or hurt. Now, suspicion settled in my mind. However, as the day was progressing, and knowing I had to return home alone, I dreaded the moment when I actually would have to take the train, so I tried to catch her attention.

"Excuse me Madam... about the job..."

"Okay. The work is not lacking. If you're ready to work, I'll soon place you wherever you want, in Paris or the province."

"I can't go to the province... George won't let me go."

"George? Oh... don't worry. I already spoke with him."

"And what did he say?"

"There's no problem. If you prefer the province, he's okay, because there's more work in the province right now."

"So, okay," I happily agreed and asked, "what do I have to do?"

"Nothing yet... just... remain as cute and nice as you are because you can meet people who have means," she said smiling while rubbing her fingers.

I smiled shyly.

"You know, I don't have much schooling."

"No worries. It's okay... Sometimes, the school of life teaches us more. You have everything you need in you," she said while her eyes looked at me up and down.

"It's true... You know, I don't have papers..."

"I know... George told me... I'll fix that. Don't worry; when I take on a girl, I take care of everything because I want her to feel good..."

"Thank you, Madam, thank you so much."

"You see, I'll make you rich in no time," she added confidently.

"I'm really lucky, Madam... thank you. What's my work exactly?"

"To do this work, you'll need a nice outfit... I will get you.... You'll receive your cash every day and I'm sure you'll make your family happy. Just look at my house to see what you can achieve..."

"Truly Madam, it's so wonderful, like the houses we see in movies."

"If you work hard, you can very quickly get an apartment like this. The only thing you have to do is to always smile and be helpful."

"Count on me, Madam Jesabel. I will not disappoint you," I said gently. "When can I start?"

"Go back home first... talk with George. Once you agree, we'll begin."

A few minutes later, filled with enthusiasm, I took leave of Jesabel after showing her my infinite gratitude and promising to do everything I could to give her satisfaction in return for everything she was doing to help me, mostly because I knew it was difficult to find a job in Europe without a work permit.

I easily found my way to the station. My train arrived quickly and I climbed aboard. It was not full, so I sat on a window seat to monitor the names of the stops, for fear of missing mine. I pinned my head languorously against the glass, thinking of my conversation with Jesabel. However, the more I thought of it, the more her wondrous promises aroused questions in me: Jesabel did not directly answer my question when I asked her what I would be doing. Money... the happiness of my family... clothing available? I suddenly had the strange sensation that important details of the extraordinary picture of my future employment had escaped me. Why would George agree to let me work far away from him, in the province, without telling me anything, since he apparently was aware of everything? What kind job could I do without a working permit in this country? I imagined myself as a maid in a hotel, a waitress or a hostess in a restaurant because I had heard that many Africans managed service companies and restaurants across France. However, Jesabel's easy lifestyle was a mark of confidence that drove away my questions. Nevertheless, I was puzzled by George's mysterious behaviour.

When I arrived home it was almost five o'clock. I went into the kitchen straight away to cook the dinner. The apartment's quiet atmosphere revived my inquisitive mood, because I still wondered why George had approved my departure from home without talking to me first. Besides, Jesabel had given me no details about my future job. What could it be exactly? What meaning should I give to her subtle answers? "I always have to be cute... Jesabel assists the girls, even those with no working permit... smile and be helpful... cash every day... the school of life!" My startled opened mouth froze suddenly. This could not be what I thought! Jesabel had never made any explicit reference or uttered offensive term, because she expected and knew that I would literally decipher her insinuations. My blood began to run cold and my limbs were trembling. I reviewed Jesabel's blank stare activated by greed and the lure of profit supporting each of the phrases she used to hold out the prospect of all the comfort I would acquire within a short spell of time: money, my family's recognition, a nice house back home... like those other girls who always came back from Europe with lots of money in less than a year. She had gone through that! In her country, she owned two houses and several cars! And, with her index finger decorated with an oversize gold ring like the rest of her fingers, she had pointed to the leather lounge we were sitting on, and had also said it was a souvenir of her period of activity. So, Jesabel was a procurer! Now, her words were banging in my head like a distant whisper. Only the grip of terror and the desire to flee could describe my emotions! It was unbelievable. So, Jesabel was recruiting me to exploit me in the sex business she had formed together with her husband and... with the support of George! I was drained: all the mercy I had formerly felt for that lady. And continuously, I repeated to myself "George! George! George!" It surely could not be my own, my George! From that moment, I wanted to push the hours on with my feet to precipitate our discussion.

Upon his return, George asked me absolutely nothing about my interview with Jesabel, which was unlike him. After all, if Jesabel was much better informed than me about what was happening in my home, there was no doubt that my partner already knew the outcome of our conversation. In any case, one thing was undeniable: now, I was afraid of him. He definitely sensed it because my reply to his silence was nothing else but painfully whispered monosyllables. I decided to take my few clothes and get away from him, like Jesabel had done with her first husband. But, by running away from George, was I not going to sink into the hell I was trying to run away from, exactly like Jesabel? I decided to confront George for once, and no matter what might happen, because I found myself in a corner.

He was sitting in front of his computer, writing his poems. Exhausted and distressed to have awaited this moment a long time, I sat on the sofa, facing and staring at him. He was not disturbed by my recurring "hem" or "bah". He also pretended not to see me at all and focused on his screen. He seemed far away, although from time to time he raised his eyes, sent me a furtive glance, then moved on with his writings. I let several minutes pass before going to the kitchen. When the dinner was ready, I served it and brought it to the dining table where we ate silently side by side like strangers sharing the same plate, with our eyes stuck on the television and listening to the news as if we were following Sunday's preaching at church. None of us dared to look the other in the eyes. I did not know who, he or I, was the most disturbed. Never, in my whole life, had I imagined I could be the victim of such atrocious action. I felt guilty indeed for partially allowing this stranger to treat me as an object by agreeing to live with him when I barely knew him, just to escape boredom back home. I had hoped that George would collect his wits quickly and cheer me up with the words I had wanted to hear so much since my return. But instead, his indifference confirmed his complicity in a plot I had first considered to have been initiated by Jesabel and her husband, a couple I found too unalike to be normal, thus raising my suspicions when I saw them together; no mark of affection was detectable in their relationship, but also because I was really surprised to see how the husband submitted to his wife.

Trembling with emotion, I muttered a few words to begin the discussion since he would not have taken any action in such circumstances, but also because it was important for me to meet his eyes to express my unconditional refusal.

"George!" I called out.

"What is it?" he said, turning to me.

"You haven't asked me how it went with Jesabel."

"Oh, I already know. She called me."

"Really?" I replied, as if surprised.

"Why are you surprised? I sent you there. You should expect me to know..."

"So you know I accepted the job!"

"Well," he said with apathy.

"But I don't know when I'm going to start. Jesabel said I must speak with you..."

"Speak about what?"

"I don't know... maybe when I could start."

"Well, whenever you want, no problem."

"How can you say 'no problem'?"

"I mean... whenever you want to leave."

"Leave?" I replied, forcing myself to stay calm.

"Yes, you're leaving Paris... you know, right?"

"No... not really... so this is what you've finally decided?"

"Yeah, I've decided!"

I was so shocked by his unexpected response that I could find no spontaneous response. I felt a burden on my shoulders, accordingly I left the table. Then, after taking heart, I pursued him:

"Why are you doing this?"

"What are you talking about?"

"When you came to my house, you found me with my parents who would never have allowed me to live with a man without being married, despite our poverty. Since I've lived with you have I ever asked you for something? Even for my trip, you made the decision, didn't you? You remember how you called me, begging me to join you here? That's why my parents and I finally agreed. Until now, I've tried to live by the rules you've set, and never complained. Even your unjustified mood changes, I bear them, your irritations and your rude words, I don't pay attention to them. I demand neither your money nor clothing. I never grumble, you know. I take whatever you want to give me. So, what's the matter? Are you trying to get rid of me? Why do you want me to work far away from you?"

George remained impassive, which upset me. Therefore I became more insistent while suppressing my anger as much as I could.

"What is it? You don't even want to answer me… Is there someone else?"

My friend persisted in a hostile silence that urged me to rise up with threatening eyes.

"You think I haven't grasped your plan? Why do you want to spoil everything between us…?"

My last question had the effect of a treacherous attack on George. He stopped me by getting up and shouting so much that I was scared of being hit.

"Are you mad? You African women, I know you well! Stop pretending to be different from others. You're only immoral flirts... and she dares speak about a relationship between *me* and her!"

When he saw that I was taken aback by the virulence of his words. He lowered his voice, "Living under my roof gives you no right... even less, to consider yourself as my partner. And I remind you that your life depends on me, so you better satisfy me as often as I want, day or night, whenever and wherever I want, because I got you out of the misery and I've saved you the ridiculous striptease your sisters offer freely at the Internet cafés to seduce white people like me. Think yourself lucky because of what I did for you... and bear in mind that you're going to pay back all the money I spent on you to the last penny..."

I certainly found it hard to believe it was George talking to me. His words were terribly disappointing. I felt helpless and deeply offended because I understood that he had decided to sacrifice me on the filthy table of sexual slavery, just like what I had heard in the past about the young Africans who were exploited in Europe because, actually, for him, I had no human value: I was black! So everything had just been a misleading illusion until now. I was completely undermined because I felt useless. I began to grumble to myself for being so blind all this time. And from that moment, I knew I could not love George the same way again. Now I wanted to protect myself from him, at least for some time, but how could I, given the influence he had on my future and, above all, the idea that he could use strength to achieve his objectives?

After that dispute, I went immediately into the bedroom, hoping that George would show some semblance of remorse to avoid a superficial relation between us. A few minutes later, I decided to ask him to let me out to look for a job, so I could pay him off little by little. So, I returned to the living room walking slowly. The dining room door was ajar. I could see George holding his mobile phone and dialling a number. It seemed that he was sending a message. It sickened me because I now understood how his mother was informed of everything! I returned to the bedroom and lay on the bed. When he later joined me, he did not touch me. Things had drastically changed between us.

When morning came, he did not go to work and stayed home all day. Never in my life had I felt so lonely! Shy tears pearled down my cheeks when I thought of my mother. Every week she was the one to praise the Lord for having blessed her house by preventing her daughter from idleness thanks to her trip to the white man's country, where money came out of the walls, where suffering did not exist, where every problem always had a solution.

What the future had in store for me, I had no idea, but I was sure of one thing: George had become arrogant and behaved hatefully to me. He refused to eat with me and declined any meal I cooked. One evening he even ordered a pizza. I would have been less affected by his attitude if he had not muttered that it was best to avoid food from an angry woman, especially from a *black*. I watched him as he was separating the pre-cut slices of the pizza topped with tomato and other tasty ingredients. Then he ate one slice after another until the last, in front of me. He left some crusts on his plate that he offered me. As I refused, he threw his plate on the floor and forced me to pick it up, which I did immediately, without opposition, because I still aspired to ease the hostilities, but also to prevent the gap between us from widening. Not being ready to take the first step towards peace anyway, I hoped that my friend would see reason and, above all, remove me from the lot of those African women who inspired in him nothing but disrespect. All in vain. His silence lasted, but proved to be nothing compared to the abyss that opened before me shortly after.

VII

The following morning at around eight o'clock, someone phoned. George answered. Then he left the house at full speed, leaving his phone on the table. Since he had awoken, he had not said a word to me, so I refrained from calling him to give it to him. However, motivated by the desire to know what he might have told his mother this time, I opened his outbox: "She knows everything. What do I do now?"

I had a doubt this message was addressed to Clarisse. I decided to check if he had received an answer: "No worries. I take care of her. xxx, Jez."

I began to tremble. I quickly put the phone down where he had left it. I rushed to the bedroom to take my few belongings and get out before George's return. But outside his energetic footsteps could be heard, getting closer and closer to the entry door. Then, followed the noise of his bunch of keys, one of which was put into the keyhole to unlock it.

George called out to me. The nervousness of his voice made me panic, so I ran to him almost without realizing it. My right little toe hit the floor so violently that I could almost believe that an invisible object had been placed there. I could not get to the parlour immediately as the throbbing pain in my foot prevented me from walking properly. Right after, while I massaged my toe, he grew impatient: "Jude is here!"

A feeling of worry spread across my chest, which I associated with my aching toe, because at the same moment the words of my grandmother sprang to my mind; one day in the village, she taught me how to recognize some warning signs that were only handed down and find their genuine meaning only in our villages: banging my foot this way just as I was going to welcome Jude meant that his visit was ominous for me. So I made a quick sign of the cross before opening the door to ward off all the bad luck he was carrying.

I threw a slightly offensive hello to Jude who pretended to be reverential in his reply. George apologized because he had to leave for a short time, which I found out later was a trick. I expressed my astonishment subtly since he had never left me at home with another man. My senses were alarmed. I dreaded that there would be unpredictable behaviour from this inscrutable gentleman. I huddled up at the end of our despicable sofa bed, leaving Jude with a large space. He sat down and faked to start a conversation with me about my family back home, my intentions and especially the development of my life with George. His mischievous attitude was imbued with embarrassment. I listened suspiciously, because this indescribable feeling that only your guts detect when danger is approaching did not leave me. It aroused in me the fear I used to feel as a teenager when passing before the stall of a seller whose cigarettes I inadvertently knocked over in the mud along the street after heavy rain. Everything in my stomach was bubbling whenever I saw him, and I could not help it, because I thought the seller would literally carry out his threat to cut off my arm if he ever grabbed me. Thinking I would never be able to escape him, I always made sure to take a short-cut to the main road to avoid passing in front of his stand. However, with time and age, I realized that his threat were mere hot air. But in this case, Jude evoked an unwanted reality that rested on no reliable justification and its values did not match with what my parents had instilled in me. As a result, I had nothing to say to him and I felt a predisposed aversion to anything that came from his mouth.

While he spoke, Jude did not mention my dialogue with his wife, which surprised me. Obviously, he also knew everything. We did not really have much to tell each other and I did not know what to expect from him, so I withdrew further into my shell. He noticed my discomfort, as well as my defensive attitude and the instability that prevented me from sitting or standing for over a minute. I was indeed moving all over the place in the living room.

"Yvette, you have no reason to be afraid of me, you know," he whispered slyly. "Come sit here," he continued, tapping the chair beside him.

That show of kindness made me fear an inappropriate gesture. Instead I sat on George's desk, avoiding turning back. His face suddenly lit up.

"Everything George is doing is for your own good... you should listen to him," he advised me.

I showed my discontent through my saddened look and my desperate expression, hoping for his understanding.

He carried on: "George isn't bad. He only wants you to be happy... you know, I underwent the same pressure he's going through at the end of every month when my wife's family asks her for money without wondering how she is earning that money. As for me, I know lots of men who wouldn't have done as much as George has already done for you. You are lucky to have met him, because he is the nicest man... the most patient, the most caring and the most understanding person I know. Let me tell you... George is a good man."

It was the same picture my dear friend had shown my parents, yet in private, the depiction of his daily life was far more demeaning if not ridiculous, but I did not want to contradict Jude despite my exasperation. I listened quietly, until the return of George who was gone for over thirty minutes. When he entered, he eluded my eyes and immediately sat near Jude, marking a distance between them and me. I watched this scene a little bewildered but still worried because this morning meeting, unfortunately, broke our routine so much that it could only augur an unsolicited surprise for me. Consequently, my negative intuition increased. George and his friend tried to mask their own uneasiness with jokes that sparked off nothing but their frozen smiles.

Afterwards, my partner launched into a tirade, as I expected, "I lost my job several weeks ago. With my poor income, I can't bear your burden any longer. And I still owe my bank all the money I borrowed for your trip. I tried, Yvette, but I can't... I can't keep you. You've already cost me not less than three thousand Euros, not to mention your frequent phone calls to your family."

"What?" I almost yelled.

Only my appalled eyes asked him why he had said nothing about his banking problems. I suddenly grasped why he had been speaking bitterly about money for some time, and especially seemed to regret the money he had paid for my trip... but never had he told me that my trip annoyed him to that extent... and him being jobless! I could hardly believe it.

"Are you taking me for a fool?" I asked him doubtfully.

"You know, it isn't easy for me, but I'm looking for a solution... the only one I've found so far to get out of trouble before things get worse, is to entrust you to Jesabel."

I was shocked that George had chosen to surrender to Mammon rather than confiding in me about his financial problems. Together we could try to face them. My eyes were fixed on the floor and did not dare turn to look at either of the two men. I was disgusted, and now dreaded the apparent outcome of this meeting.

George had always been so respectable with me that sometimes I felt guilty about not being able to give him back what he had offered me. Meanwhile, my heart swelled with pain, which was ultimately betrayed by my eyes blurring with tears that I soon wiped away with the back of my hand. I now regretted my previous life, because I honestly expected infinite happiness in France. I unfortunately now realized that my life in my country was much more enviable despite the absence of the material comfort I enjoyed in France: since my arrival, I had lived almost like a hermit and my partner's behaviour had not helped me integrate. I had eventually lost all joy in life. Even the smile had deserted my lips and nostalgia only made me brood about unachievable projects all day long. What was worse, I had put my life in the hands of a man whose love had clearly reached its limits. In his eyes, I was nothing but a waste of time. Now he had decided to get rid of me. But, to accomplish his crafty design, he used his cowardice to forge a false reality about our disagreement.

I was more unsettled than ever because nobody had told me that, in France, the solidarity we knew in my country did not apply here, at least not in the way I had imagined. Because my parents lived in the city, we regularly welcomed some cousins, uncles or aunts for several months at home without being irritated or changing our habits. Some of them even stayed for years to study, and sometimes, my parents were naturally forced to look after them as if they were their own kids. Also, it was not uncommon to see foreigners settle in a village or a town, penniless, remain there long enough to start their own family and eventually be merged with the natives: that was the way our Ghanaian hairdresser established herself. I was having trouble understanding what was happening. So many ideas running through my head: I was a stranger in France, but I was thinking about the white people who came to start a new life in my country and the way we admired them. I thought of how all the doors were open and their applications were accepted, even before they had made them, just to enable them to get an easy start. George was now showing me such disregard, in front of Jude too, that it changed my whole vision of this country that I had so much desired. Nevertheless, I was sure to have enough resources to get out of it. So I commanded George to speak his mind. He did so bluntly, "Jude is taking you to your new home!"

I was dazed by his eyes devoid of expression. My mouth was left gaping for over a minute. I was not ready for this separation.

"George, I beg you", I yelled many times. "You can't do this… you can't let me go like this."

It was in vain. George could hear me no more.

"Gather your stuff, because our paths are now parted…"

"George, please, you can't make me go with him…"

He went immediately to the room to pack my clothes in an old gym bag, ten items in total and my two pairs of shoes. He then went into the bathroom where he also took my towel worn by multiple washes, and my toothbrush. He came back to the dining room. He handed me the bag without hesitation. The Bible I had brought from my country was missing, so he went to fetch it and handed it to me. I pressed it against my chest while walking towards the door, followed by his friend.

Jude took me to his black car with tinted windows, while tears were filling my eyes. Two white men were already in the back seat. One of them opened the door when we approached and invited me to sit next to the one who had remained inside, and then he got in and sat next to me.

George stayed in the apartment. I imagined him watching us from his window: owing to his lack of courage, he could not withstand the dramatic scene engraved on my face. I refused to burst into tears in front of the coldness and callousness of my partner who had just given a different direction to my destiny. Only the unknown worried me, so my quiet moans began to thunder more and more and I could not hold them back any longer. But this did not seem to bother Jude.

He did not speak to me throughout the journey, except when I stopped lamenting a bit about my fate. Later, he tried to be nice and murmured baseless phrases as if speaking to himself. I realized with disgust that George's power was formidable and undoubtedly the most destructive, as he had managed to get me to come to him, offered me unparalleled kindness to disarm me of any suspicion and finally he had thrown me into depravity. What upset me the most, to my greatest sorrow, was the thought that George had been plotting my ruin for a long time, because he had offered me the opportunity to come to Europe. He had been concocting this cowardly and wicked plan with my fellow African. The man whose human side and social vision had provoked in me a growing love, dramatically amplifying my feelings, had become indifferent to his own immoral action and cared not one bit about the great pain he was inflicting upon me.

The trip seemed infinite, which increased my fears. I sketched different plans to run away whenever the car would slow down due to heavy traffic. But I was surrounded by these strangers. In my mind was the omnipresent image of my mother: what was I going to tell her now? She had so much confidence in George. Only abundant tears running down my cheeks answered me. At that time, I also realized that I was being thrown into a vicious circle that George had just triggered. I did not know what to expect but I did long to reach our destination to relieve my unbearable anxiety.

When we got in front of a poorly maintained building in on area of Paris I had never been before, Jude asked me to get out of the car. The brick building was six stories high and from outside it appeared uninhabited since, at that time of day, all the windows facing the street were closed. Jude walked in front of me and gallantly held the door with one hand to let me in while carrying my suitcase with his other hand. I proceeded nervously into the deserted lobby where I noticed there were no mailboxes. Jude asked me to use the stairs in front of us. I obeyed. We climbed to the fifth floor and found two doors, one on the left of the stairs and another on the right. He pulled a key from his pocket and opened the one on the right, then invited me to enter. We were greeted by a large single room simply furnished with a double bed and a small dresser. Not long after, someone knocked at the door. As I thought, it was Jesabel. Her presence pacified me as much as it terrified me because, in a way, she was confirming the pitiful fate awaiting me from that moment on.

Jesabel came closer to me. Her smooth skin coated with some golden glitter powder made her face sparkle and her expression was as serious as the time I met her in her living room. She turned around to look at me like a victorious predator, without opening her mouth. Then she stood before me. Her bovine and unruffled eyes seemed to lack any glimmer of lucidity. She licked her blood-red lips, and later took a few steps back while continuing to watch me. I tried to look her straight in the eyes without frowning, to enable her to read dejection in mine. Jesabel's remained firmly superior until the end of her initial check-up that unfortunately led me to realize the irrefutable truth that I was nothing else but her employee, a prostitute. She finally opened her mouth to talk: the two last floors of the building belonged to her; I would soon meet my new companions, "the other girls". She sounded formal. So I suddenly lost hope: the assistance that I had expected even in a supernatural way since my departure from George's apartment had not shown up. Worst of all, my African sister finally unveiled the true face hiding behind the pretty facade topped with a short wig she wore perfectly: George had handed her my passport! For the very first time I caught a flash of a slight sincere sentiment in her voice when she said, almost like a propitious promise, that she would help me to update my residence permit to get me out of hiding, which made my heart rejoice, erasing some fear that had seized my entire body just before. In the moment that followed, Jesabel staggered me with the news that she had paid George about five thousand Euros for my services. I belonged to her now! And for the three years to come, I would have to work for her, in order to reimburse that sum. Her austere voice numbed all my limbs as I realized that horror and decadence had indeed settled in my life.

I froze in panic, thinking that I had not come to France for this. What would I tell my mother? What would become of me? What did she expect me to do with the thong and the lace bodystocking she had given me? I had often seen such things in catalogues at home, but I had never worn any before. Jude, who was sitting on a chair in a corner of the room near the door, watched me strip to try them on to obey my new mistress! Once again, I could not restrain the tears gushing from my eyes as I dropped down my long pleated skirt. Then I took off my shirt and my underwear and I laid them on the bed. I took Jesabel's outfit and clumsily put them on, so she helped me. Then she took some steps back to observe me again, then verbally appreciated the effect of those pieces of fabric on my body, while her husband, nervously passing his hand through his crew-cut hair as if the scalp was itching, nodded. As he saw that I had seen him, he forced a smile on his thin lips, whereas his elusive blue eyes externalized his naïveté. I understood why he had never inspired in me anything but antipathy: in front his wife, the ambitious and driven young man who flirted and tried to flatter me with George's support had been replaced by a cautious, opportunistic and hypocritical man. How I wished to pour the visceral anger of my guts on the villain who was as guilty, if not more so, as George! His eyes were set on mine and I ascertained that he read my hatred. It was unbearable to him, so he turned his gaze away while Jesabel came towards me once again. I jumped when she leaned over the bed where I sat with arms firmly crossed to cover my half naked body. She took my clothes and gave them to Jude.

"Room temperature's good. You'll remain just so," she said.

It was appalling. In my family, modesty was part of education. Never had I walked around a house all day long without any other clothes on but a thong and bodystocking. I stood up, both hands joined, to beg Jesabel to give me at least my blouse, but she refused and added that it would be pointless since I would soon receive my first client who was on his way. On hearing these last words, I burst into tears. My hands were pressed against my eyes to prevent me from seeing the horrible scenes that had overwhelmed my broken wits. I also kept my elbows as tight as possible to my chest to hide my breasts. Then I dug my head in between my knees that were already wet with tears and remained in this position for some time, crying loudly and unceasingly calling my parents and even my late grandmother for her mystical release from the hands of Jesabel and Jude, who, during that time, inspected every corner including the dresser's drawers. I ended up wearing myself out and my voice began to fade, so I stopped crying.

Suddenly, there was another knock at the door. My nervousness grew, thinking it was the client. Instead, a young African lady came in, dressed like me. I was rather relieved to see another individual in my situation, because I knew she had to occupy one of the neighbouring apartments to afford to walk around almost naked. By the way Jesabel spoke to her in a language I did not understand, I was sure she had come to cheer me up. In fact I needed a friend, any kind soul able to guess my confusion. The young lady stammered fairly inaccurate French mixed with English words so that it required patience to follow what she was saying. Additionally, her extreme submission to Jesabel instantly raised a hint of suspicion and I forgot my previous idea that I could become her ally. Without needing to know her more, my distrust slid into an uncontrollable aversion when she began to give me advice at the request of Jesabel who threw a quick glance at the bathroom. A reassuring flash lit up her cold face when she promised to come over every week, and asked me to be a good girl to make things easy. Then she opened the door, let the young lady out first, then her husband who carried away my suitcase. She followed them and locked the door behind her.

I had neither the strength to cry, nor voice to scream. I fell hard on the bed, cursing George and his promises as well as the poverty that had made me dream so much of a better life in France. I remembered my friends back home who would have done the impossible to be in my place right now. If only they knew... And my parents who expected the announcement of my impending marriage with *him* any time, a sign of my final move towards a social status which, in turn, would give them the esteem, but especially the affluence that they had hoped for all these years. Indeed, Jesabel had assured me I would soon make people in my country jealous by making big money! But I had not come to France to earn that kind of money, money that forever would sully my life as a woman and frightened me to death. However, with no prospect of escaping this dirty lucrative experience, I had to resign myself to it without resistance.

VIII

The first night I spent in my new place was terribly stressful. An unknown man came into the room I occupied at around eight o'clock. The door was opened by a lady I was seeing for the first time and who knew my name. The man, about forty years old, seemed to be a regular since he noticed I was new. He wished to know where I used to work before, but I refrained from responding so as not to give him the pleasure of pride for being my first client. Even forced to abandon my body to this stranger, I was determined to keep at least my thoughts and my past dignity because it was the only thing that would remain of my privacy. So, I listened to him talking about himself as long as he wished until he undressed. He stayed in the room overnight, rejoicing in practising his fantasies. As for me, bruised, I submissively let him, relying solely on the minute that would end my mental and physical torture. When he had finished what he had paid for, the stranger fell asleep next to me; so, almost lifeless, I found some respite.

I loathed the briny smell of his sweaty skin so much that I had severe nausea. I went to the bathroom to vomit, but in vain. All my limbs were aching as if I had been tied up. I rinsed my face casually over the sink and, walking slowly, I returned to the room where the man was lying on his back, snoring. Between the door and the bed, a halogen lamp diffused its filtered light across the bedroom. Part of the stranger's face was lit up. I looked at him a few minutes without moving, trembling from head to toe. I could not take my eyes away from his topless and hairy chest while my feet were dragging me to the lamp without wishing to. Horror and disgust won over the pit of my isolation. This stranger had opened the fatal abyss of my obvious affliction. I firmly grabbed the foot of the lamp and walked towards the bed. The veiled light illuminated his pinkish complexion. His repugnant breath only increased my disgust. I lifted up my arm, ready to get rid of this despicable image. Suddenly, I saw my silhouette over the lying man. I got scared. My legs began to bend and my hand trembled so hard that the light dropped. I only just caught it and then very gently put it back in its place. I walked to the foot of the bed where I sat, weeping quietly and reviving in my mind the instructions of my parents, who, since childhood had taught us never to express our anger with violence. My heart swelled at the thought, but I had to calm myself down and take my time: a chance to run away would appear one day! That was better than a crime. Finally, I escaped the room for a few hours, when sleep took me.

In the early morning, while I was still at the foot of the bed, the individual stood up, eager to leave the room. Before going, he put a few notes on the dresser as a tip because my boss had been paid in advance, as usual.

Once he was out of the room, I shouted myself hoarse to the point of losing my voice. The lady who had brought him in rushed into my room to reprimand me because my sobs were bothering everyone. The night before, I had not noticed her imposing size or the harsh features of her acned face stripped with lightening products. She asked me to cry silently if I intended to wail all day. Then, as if captured by a small feeling of guilt, she told me to take a shower; she would bring me my breakfast if I wanted. Not wishing to fuel the thirst for violence readable in her eyes by any means, I clenched my teeth knowing that my future lay in her hostile hands.

I had no strength to eat because I just wanted to feel the water run over my skin in the hope of scrubbing off the stain that first night had imprinted on my body and forever in my head. Without answering my interlocutor whose name I still did not know, I slowly pushed open the door of the bathroom with one hand while with the other I was trying to cover my chest. I stayed about an hour in the shower, almost enjoying the sweetness of warm water slipping down my body which I tried to exfoliate with my hands and soap. Dissatisfied with the result, I wrapped my thong around my hand and soaped myself all over again while rubbing the lace with such force that I felt I was skinning myself in some places. Despite that, I was not relieved: the pain I felt at the bottom of my heart and in my limbs tirelessly reminded me of the atrocious turn of my fate.

After showering, I sat on the bed. I was shivering due to coldness or hatefulness, either way it made no difference. I pulled one of the soiled bed sheets and I wrapped it around my body despite the stench that brought to my mind the horror of the nightly frolics. For long minutes, I remained seated, drained, with downcast eyes. When I turned myself towards the dresser, I noticed that the money the client had left was gone. I looked away as I was now dazed, indifferent, and too concerned about the pain that was torturing my insides.

The daunting lady came into my room and handed me a tray with my morning meal. I asked her if she had taken the money. For an answer I received a blow. It was so sudden that I did not have time to catch the plate which had flown out of my hands. Finally, she forbade me to ask her questions and told me she would bring me new bed sheets and clean clothes in a few minutes. As she was leaving the room, she advised me to pick up the scrambled eggs scattered on the floor before they got cold and clean the floor. This latest incident only worsened my state. I looked around me, hoping to find an escape route. But the window was blocked. Therefore, I considered that only death was my relief. As a matter of fact, I started wishing it with all my strength, expecting it to drag me out of this hell. But the thought of my mother made me instinctively abandon this fatal idea.

I cleaned the studio without eating anything. I had barely finished when the lady brought me a lace bodystocking, whereas I desired suitable clothes to hide my dishonoured body. She told me that another client would come in less than an hour, so I had to get ready quite quickly to welcome him. Despite my tears and entreaties, she left, slamming the door behind her. She returned ten minutes later, this time accompanied by the young woman I had seen the day before. She said that the lady would stay with me for some time. I realized it was a ploy to give me the strength to cope. The woman introduced herself as Bridget. I calmed down a bit, because with her at least I could talk.

"How are you feeling?"

"My body hurts... everywhere. I also have a headache."

"You must eat well, otherwise you will not hold out... take this, this will help."

"What's that?"

"A little something that will soon get you back into shape."

Thus, without knowing it, I began using a soft drug that I swiftly became dependent on because it allowed me to forget all my troubles, both physical and psychological, and to please the regular clients I was assigned day and night, at a rampant rate. As a daily routine, I was getting a dozen that often left me tips. Since Bridget had warned me of the lack of scruples of the austere, intimidating lady who also happened to be our governess, I took care to hide all the money I received from my clients under the mattress, sometimes in the chest or in the bathroom's waste bin. After one week, I found myself with about a thousand Euros, earned by my body supported by the drug. When Jesabel came to visit me two weeks later, seeing no tears in my eyes was enough for her to conclude that my learning period, if that was what it was, was going well. She did not ask me anything but said that I was fit and promised to soon allow me out of the building from time to time, like the other girls.

I had been working for Jesabel for over three weeks. One day, the governess, who looked after the girls in the absence of the mistress, and treated them rather unceremoniously, submitting them to the most atrocious acts like a crooked foreman, told me that I was allowed to leave, but I was going to be escorted by two people, a man and a woman I had never seen before. This was also the only time since I had left George's home that I was permitted to wear decent clothes. After recommending that I behave myself if I did not want something unpleasant to happen to me, my coaches led me, at my request, to the nearest post office. I bought a phone card to call my parents because I was afraid they were very worried about my silence. Then, helped by the accompanying lady, I carried out my first money transfer to my family.

On the phone, my mother was very pleased to hear that George had found me a full-time moonlighting job, which now left me little time to call her as regularly as I did in the past. When she asked me about my fiancé, I replied "everyone is fine" to avoid lying to her or involuntarily confessing the truth. I stopped her questions by talking of the money sent that she could cash as soon as we ended our conversation. Much more than Bridget's honeyed words, my mother's exultant voice was a solace to me. I also spoke to my father who thanked me for thinking of them, because, he added, some people get lost once they cross the Mediterranean. I then thought that if he could only imagine what I endured daily, he would know why these people vanish, when they had the chance. I felt so dirty that I would have opted to fade away into oblivion as the circumstances of my confinement actually enabled me to, but my conscience was stronger.

My hour and a half break ended as quickly as it began. Underfed because of my daily lack of appetite, my body visibly withered, and when I saw my reflection in the window of a building adjacent to the post office, I was almost shocked: I was floating in my own skinny clothes and my cheeks gave me a depressed appearance. I felt so bad that I almost started crying, but I held back my tears. My escort took me back at the time fixed by the governess who led me into my cold studio where she asked me to give her the clothes I was wearing and get ready for my next visitor. I had a headache because of my retained tears but also owing to the smell of the room that filled my nostrils and almost suffocated me since the only time it was ventilated a bit was when the door was open, mostly when I received a new depraved client. I pulled back the heavy curtain that prevented the air from circulating properly in the room, unfortunately behind it there was a tilt and turn window without any latch which was locked from the outside by iron bars. The escaping solution that I had just imagined was terminated as suddenly as it had appeared to me, since I could not even open the window.

My days were routine. Nothing new ever happened. Thus, boredom mixed with the repulsion of my situation made me lose all hope of getting out. The only time I really rested was when I allowed to leave the building, always with one or two guards. Sometimes, Bridget joined me to keep me company. Because she had been in the house for a very long time, she helped me cope, especially thanks to her miraculous pills.

Her moral support was vital to me in this no-win situation, although, like me, she had no secret recipe and could not promise me a better future away from the building: we were both illegal and we were reminded every day that whoever tried to run away would be caught, if the police did not catch us first. So we had a rather limited choice: returning back home and bearing the humiliation that would accompany it or forcible confinement and the compulsory use of our body for money.

Still, I never saw Bridget complain. I guessed she was in her thirties, and later, she told me that Jesabel, actually her cousin, had brought her to France three years earlier to work as a babysitter with a French family. However, upon arrival, Jesabel had shut her up for several months in a room where she regularly received men who assaulted her to satisfy their whims. She ended up drugged, alone and helpless. With time, she became accustomed to the life she did not like at first because of the money she was making, to the extent that she could not imagine herself doing something else such as working hard in an office or as a maid to earn in a month what she could get in a few days. She had now accepted her new life and insisted I should do the same because this would make me suffer less while making my family happier. As for her, the money she earned was paying for the university fees of her brother and some cousins, as well as feeding her family. She was considering going back to get her nine-year-old daughter once she had her residence permit. She had so many projects in mind, and the time that had elapsed since her arrival in France did not matter as she was certain to catch up by using her hidden savings.

She spoke very little of her cousin, "Sista Jez" as she called her, and nothing in her voice betrayed the resentment she felt for this sister who had deliberately pushed her into this decadence after having drugged her for fear that she would run away. As she knew I was a neophyte in the business, whenever we could, she did her best to teach me useful tricks to get more tips, to learn how to distinguish good clients from bad ones. She advised me continuously and ensured I was using the condoms the governess frequently put in the bedside cabinet. Actually, that was the only thing we were granted as required, without complaining, since even communication between the girls was virtually banned. So, I felt very lucky to have Bridget's friendship. She also informed me that a dozen girls were in the building and, like me, all belonged to Jesabel. Most were newly arrived from Africa and were left to fend for themselves without resources, having been thrown out by family members refusing to accommodate them; however, others, more independent and determined to succeed, had voluntarily offered their services to Jesabel to avoid being on the streets. For that reason, they received a salary determined with the boss, in addition to their tips from clients.

She also told me that, after a while, if I was fortunate, Jesabel might decide to let me work outdoors. When I tried to find out more, Bridget was more explicit.

"Sista Jez regularly sends girls to work in the provinces or at the Swiss border. And… those who want to escape often end up trying their luck. You know, most of the time the girls are so dependent that for fear of being caught, they prefer to remain with Jez. In all cases, once we leave this place, there is more freedom."

"What do I need to do to have a chance to be sent outdoors?"

"It actually depends on how you behave daily."

With the idea of a possible outdoor life, I determined to work hard, bearing all the whims of my regulars, just in the hope of hearing them brag about my submission to the boss. Some days my body was suffering the tortures of unscrupulous clients who never failed to bring their own tools of pleasure. One of them tried to hit me with a whip, but I objected. Unfortunately, he left me no tip, but when leaving, he hastened to produce a negative report to the governess. She rushed into my studio while I was washing in the shower. She flung me a lash of whip that surprised me so much that I uttered a shrill cry, which infuriated her more. She then scolded me for several minutes, and insulted me without asking me anything at all, then commanded me to learn to be more obedient otherwise she herself would take responsibility for my education. I came out of the bathroom with my face wet with water and tears. I had the impression that whatever I did only turned into a catastrophe. How could I survive in this foreign land where nobody understood me? This life was not worth the effort! My parents had never laid a hand on me whenever I had done wrong, even as a child; they had always reasoned and explained things to me. So why should I endure such atrocities?

I was still lamenting when Bridget burst into my room too, furious. She blamed me for turning down my last client. Her French that was already difficult to interpret, it was now more incomprehensible than ever. Puzzled, I tried to guess the reason for her anger. Shortly after, she became as protective as usual and said, "You're not allowed to turn down a client who has paid..."

"I did everything he asked me to, but I refused to be whipped," I said, quite agitated.

Bridget was interested in hearing my story because the client had told the governess that he had spent the time cajoling me into doing what he asked me to because I did not want to be touched. As a result, feeling wronged, he had demanded repayment of the sum he had paid. And as he started to shout in the hall, the governess agreed to pay back half the money to calm him down.

I suddenly had the feeling of having been doubly deceived: a stranger came to own my body, had lied to avoid paying the price, then had left freely while I was punished. Bridget pretended to believe me and left. I was more depressed, if it was still possible, and I felt sorry for myself: once again, this event had succeeded in making my body almost as soft as a snail. Death, my only possible solution to the growing nightmare I could never get used to, hovered around me. But I lacked courage. I had neither the strength nor the right to end my life: my family was counting on me! I now decided to pursue my efforts to win the governess's grace, because, in her criminal hands, there lay a possible exit and, perhaps my hope of escape.

Eight long months passed in the building, more serenely than in the beginning. The governess had become less severe with me as I cried less, and she decided to reward my good behaviour by a promotion, setting the number of clients attending my bedroom to three per day. I appreciated her initiative because from that moment, I only received clients I already knew. This change relieved me because it now spared me from the excessive desires of adventurous and unscrupulous newcomers.

However, one morning, the governess sent me a new customer. Submissive like a slave in front of her fearless foreman, I accepted this assignment half-heartedly. I was angry and could not hide my hostility for being so naive as to believe that the frightening lady would respect her commitments vis-à-vis me.

An attractive man of medium height with the silhouette of a hidalgo came into my room at the time indicated. He probably was around sixty. His elegant clothes and politeness showed he was wealthy, which wiped out my frustration about receiving him. He cast a quick glance around the room, rolling his big brown eyes like marbles, before looking at me. He was wearing a dark suit and a beige shirt that mitigated the appearance of his blotchy complexion. He came closer to me, one hand in his pocket, the other holding an unlit cigar; and with much reserve, he sat on the bed next to me, though I was staring into space. I did not react, waiting for his appeals.

"What's your name?" He asked with a serious but slow voice.

"Yvette," I answered without turning towards him.

"I'm Richard."

Then he began to undress. When he was naked, I lay down on the bed, offering him my body naturally.

After that visit, Richard became a regular, coming several days in a week. In the beginning, he came in the morning. I did not dare to ask him questions, so I often imagined that he had just left a lovely wife who gave him his breakfast, kissed him goodbye and wished him a good day when they parted to go to their respective work places. He was very courteous and patient with me. It was the first time a client seemed human in the way he treated me, showing some interest in my welfare. So I began to hope for his presence each time I was ordered to get ready for the next client, because I loved the smell of his lightly scented skin and the pleasant fragrance of his grey and silky hair.

After more than a month, Richard booked me for a whole weekend. I was delighted by this news when the governess confirmed it one Friday evening, after Jesabel had agreed to allow me to leave the building because she knew him well. The idea of spending two days away from the studio seemed to be a paradise, even if I was nervous about what would happen. That night, the governess spent more than an hour in my room to prepare me for the outing, but she also warned me not to get sidetracked, because she would sooner or later know how I had behaved.

The next morning, Richard arrived at around eight o'clock. He waited for me in his car. I was escorted outside by the governess, whose eyes were tarnished with suspicion. Richard was leant back on a black car parked at the entrance of the building. He opened the passenger door. I anxiously got in without looking back, knowing the greedy governess was behind me. Richard also jumped in, and nodding good-bye to the governess, he drove off.

I had two days of recreation. The most enjoyable and intimate time I could remember of all my dissolute life. My client, Richard, took me to his detached house, an hour's drive from Paris. He showed me a smaller room than his, but joined me whenever he desired me. Our frolics were without fantasy as Richard's sexual appetite was not excessive. So, we spent much time chatting. He never failed to comment on my performance, but what fascinated him the most was my quietness and my extraordinarily sad eyes. He wanted to hear my story, but I deliberately avoided talking about myself, remembering the governess's warning, but also because I had learnt that I should not trust anyone, especially when they were close to Jesabel. Thus, he told me his own, bit by bit: he was running an insurance company founded by his late father. He did not really work, because he had been forced to take over as the only heir, since all his family members were dead. I was stunned to hear such a thing and asked him how he managed to withstand the immense void caused by this condition because it was inconceivable for me to live alone, with no one to relate to. He explained that he travelled a lot and his friends were somehow his family. Moreover, as he could easily feel weary in a relationship, he had never married to avoid any permanent relationship with anyone. Even if he sometimes felt alone, he loved his freedom. That was why he was moved by the anxiety he read in my eyes from his first visit because it reminded him of the fear he episodically suffered when extreme loneliness made him vulnerable. However, recognizing his selfish nature, he wanted me by his side throughout the weekend because he did not want to be alone. His speech touched me, and despite the Eden-like environment in which we were, I had to force myself not to reveal to Richard all my suffering. So I kept repeating to myself that he had paid to have me exclusively and I should not behave in a different way. No familiarity was allowed with the client! So I accomplished my mission in a professional manner, taking advantage of the fragile and ephemeral happiness that the distance from the Parisian studio brought about.

The escapade ended too soon unfortunately. Richard took me back to the governess at the scheduled time. I found myself momentarily plunged into a depression as soon as I arrived. I called Bridget. She came into my room, reluctantly and less talkative than usual. I told her about my weekend, revealing my interest for this man who treated me better than any client had ever done. Bridget warned me to stay on my guard because I could be deeply disappointed if I was dreaming of a special relationship with Richard. She did not stay with me long, but before leaving my studio, she asked whether I had received a tip, which I confirmed, stating that Richard had given me five hundred Euros that I was going to send to my family whenever I was next allowed to go out. She was definitely not as cheerful as usual. I asked her to sell me a small dose of the little pills that always made me feel great. She pulled a small bottle out of her bra, slipped a pill in the palm of her hand and then handed it to me. I stared in astonishment as she generally provided a weekly dose. I gave her money without saying anything and watched her leaving quite gloomy.

Once alone, I added Richard's generous bonus to the plastic bag I used as a provisional purse that I regularly hid in different places in the room. This time I placed it between the mattress and the bed base. It was about three thousand Euros and I rejoiced because I could use that money one day, if ever I was no longer in that place.

I had the immense pleasure of receiving no visitor the rest of the day, which allowed me to continue to delight in the moments shared with Richard. In the evening, I was sent a client and I resumed my activities incessantly until the morning. When I was freed from my obligations, I asked the governess for permission to call my parents. She agreed and sent two people to come with me as expected. Before leaving, I took out six hundred Euros from my hiding place and concealed the rest behind the dresser.

I talked a few minutes with my mother in a phone booth. She blessed me many times for the large sum of money I had sent them that would enable them to live comfortably for several months. Our conversation ended quickly. Though I appreciated it, I still felt like screaming for help. However, no sound but a whimper of agony came out of my mouth. I breathed a big blow to hold back the tears caused by the flood of questions that disheartened me when I thought of running away, but realized that I was very much afraid of living out of the building now! The governess kept repeating that whoever went over the threshold without authorization would be killed before walking one hundred metres. Besides, having no one to welcome me, taking such a risk was too dangerous. I chose life, despite my affliction and my humiliation.

I did not stay out long because the governess had granted me only thirty minutes. And when I returned to my studio, new underwear was waiting for me on the bed. No longer ashamed to undress, I handed my clothes to my escort lady who left immediately. A customer arrived shortly after and, although I was exhausted, I had to satisfy him for his money. He left me a little tip of thirty Euros that I decided to store in my purse after his departure. When I pulled the dresser, I had a strange feeling that I was mistaken: my purse was not there! Doubting my memory of the place where I had put it, I removed the mattress from the bed and threw it on the floor. Nothing! I ran to look behind the toilet in the bathroom. Nothing! I opened the drawer of the bedside cabinet on the right side of the bed: only packages of condoms, tissues, a few papers, but no purse. My legs went wobbly and I fell backwards onto the bed's hard slats and immediately felt a pain in my lower back that I ignored due to the shock of my missing purse. I wanted to scream "Why?" but I lacked strength. Who could rob me this way, while I thought I was finally accepted in this ruthless place? Everyone earned their tips by the sweat of their body, so why would someone steal mine? My first thought accused Bridget, but the governess came to my mind immediately.

Yet, I had tried to stay away from other girls, just to avoid a camaraderie that could cause me problems with one or the other. I could not banish from my mind the idea that only the governess had access to the various apartments. And she had already been equally mean to me. I called for Bridget and explained my misfortune to her counting on her friendly support to help me find my vanished money. This time, she was even more distant. She did not ask any questions as she typically did spontaneously. Nevertheless, she promised to enquire discreetly so as not to worsen the governess's already bad mood. Then she returned to her room leaving me devastated and in tears, but before that and to my amazement, she tidied mine to allow me to be ready for any upcoming appointment.

Soon after, Bridget and the governess were both standing on my doorstep! The first accused the second of stealing my money. I was dumbfounded by such a misleading accusation, but even more by this behaviour that I did not expect. I undertook to answer Bridget's offensive allusion to clarify the situation and make clear to the governess that Bridget was trying to save her skin for the theft she must have definitely committed. The governess barely listened to me; having become unspeakably incensed, she literally threw all her weight on me and started beating me up, hitting my head and insulting me. Her attack was so impulsive that I fell on the floor, and crossed my hands over my head to protect it. I was shouting and calling Bridget for help. The young lady remained at the door that she closed to stifle my cries, with her arms folded across her chest.

After a few minutes, she ordered the governess to stop and she immediately did. I was on the floor some time, sobbing, not for pain or for my bloodied nose, but for the abrupt and shocking scene that had just happened. At least it made me understand that Bridget certainly stole my money, therefore she probably was not what she claimed to be, which increased my anger, as I really thought she was my friend. How could she be so filthy, as she had always been honest with me before?

The governess left the room while Bridget approached me.

"Your money, you can forget it," she whispered sadly. "You've won the top prize... where you're going, you'll not need it... you're leaving in a few days," she continued.

Bridget's graceful voice was imbued with a disdain that I would have never imagined. If someone had told me she would be so cold and arrogant one day, I thought I would have denied she could behave like that, especially with me. I did not really understand what she was trying to tell me and I willingly blamed her coarse accent that was more pronounced because of the irritation that made her wild and at the same time conveyed an extreme dislike that prevented me from speaking to her. Moreover, Bridget was now one of my foes as a result of her exposed selfishness, and having learnt to avoid being the target of my enemies, I tried not to express my contempt, so as not to give her another excuse to harm me, or take the risk of losing Jesabel's support as she seemed to have gradually softened. So I looked at her without a word all the time she spoke, showing me the flames of her fiendish jealousy and bitterness. Naturally, it was to my advantage not to disclose the matter of the theft. Then, very quietly, while listening, I went to my bathroom to clean my bruised face, and I noticed that she had followed me, but not to assist me.

"Yeah, you need to be beautiful, baby," she said casually. "Some Richard paid big money to Jesabel for you. So you'll soon leave us... some still have the chance to ensnare rich whites," she said sourly, then turned on her heels and walked away!

IX

Richard picked me up one afternoon, to my greatest joy. I was so happy to see him, my liberator, that I inwardly thanked Heaven a thousand times. I began to dream of a re-discovery of my emotional desires. Renewal and joy had finally banged on my door with this good-looking man who drove me to his apartment in a posh Parisian neighbourhood. I longed to know why he had decided to get me out of that damaging life when he did not know me and had had the opportunity to meet other girls before me.

We arrived in Richard's huge apartment, on the third floor of an old building. It had a wonderful view of the Eiffel Tower and was partially lit by shy rays of sunlight that broke in through a balcony decorated with creepers. I went closer to admire the most beautiful picture of Paris I had ever seen, even in the movies I used to watch. I stood still for a few seconds, appreciative and looked totally elated. I thought that, after all this time, finally, I was in Paris. Nostalgia and questioning had come to an end, for life was opening a new chapter where everything was now accessible because I was free. Therefore I was able to take initiatives and change my future.

Afterwards, Richard made me take a tour of the apartment in a formal way. It was as spacious as a whole house in my country, with three bedrooms and a tastefully furnished living room. The open-plan main room led on to the balcony. In the middle of this room stood a large lounge with a beige leather sofa and a glass coffee table where a few magazines had been carefully laid; and above the table, a large upscale television was mounted into the wall. On the left, a dining room with four chairs around the table upon which stood a jar filled with fresh roses. Richard offered me one after smelling it, which I supposed to be his way of welcoming me into his home. I thanked him and followed him into the kitchen where the nicely ordered and modern equipment moved me as I thought I was in one of those houses we had only seen on television. At a glance, I liked its heavy cherry wood cupboards and its brightness. Without lingering, Richard showed me the bathroom and the toilet I could use as well as the closed door of his bedroom, where he said he had his own bathroom and dressing-room. Afterwards, we went to my bedroom: there was a large double bed perfectly made with bicolour linens matching the beige floral wallpaper. In one corner, a chair and a wardrobe in solid teak on which was mounted a large mirror. The harmony and the sweet smell of the room pacified me, so I felt relaxed. Richard opened the wardrobe, where I was surprised to discover a dozen new dresses hanging. I was filled with emotion and thanked him greatly. However, his rather dry response made me understand straight away that I should consider my presence in his house as temporary, because I was just a stranger to him. It affected me to some extent only, because I felt that I would be able to make him change his mind thanks to my loving disposition and my desire to live great moments in his company and for extricating me from the hell of exploitation. Even if he did not love me at that moment, as long as he would not submit me to depravity like George, I had enough love to share and to ripen the fruit of passion in our relationship.

In the evening, Richard asked me to wear one of the stylish outfits he had bought me and took me to dinner at a chic restaurant where the cutlery was so heavy that at every bite I fear my fork would fall on the floor. Chandeliers hanging from the ceiling illuminated the room, giving a fantastic brightness to the lavish decor and furnishings. People's eyes on me were heavy to bear. Internally, I first blamed my way of walking when we entered, then my attitude that was forever marked by my wretched past. But worse than that, being so noticeable and far from the four walls that had hidden the shameful activities so cruelly imposed on me for nearly a year made me paranoid: I saw a potential client in all the males looking at me. I was afraid of being addressed when I met the eyes of some of them. I consequently tried to focus my attention on Richard when I dared to look up. And despite all his paternalistic efforts, I was not able to overcome my discomfort, especially when I noticed that I was the only African in the room. I ate very little, leaving more than half of the jugged hare Richard had recommended. Finding his intention appropriate, I followed his suggestion, thinking that it would remind me of the delicious game that we often enjoyed during the few trips my parents, my brothers, my sister and I spent in the village. When my discomfort became almost unbearable, Richard showed himself once again very chivalrous in agreeing to take me home.

Upon our return, he accompanied me to the door of my bedroom, which was separated from his by a long corridor that divided the apartment into two so that we could have lived together without interfering with one another. However, while hoping to spend the first full night in the arms that strengthened and protected me from the excesses of Jesabel's guards, Richard withdrew after wishing me good night. Despite my slight disappointment, I was soothed. I decided to go to bed straight away, waiting to see what the next day had in store for me.

At dawn, when I was still fast asleep, Richard came into my room, stripped naked and uninhibited. He woke me up vigorously, to make love, energized by the aphrodisiac he regularly used, as I was going to realize much later. Surprisingly, the man I had known presented me with a new face: he was now domineering and unemotional. He possessed my body in a beastly way as ever, then, having satisfied his libido, he left me on the bed as exhausted as I used to be after a day of work at my old studio. Shortly after that, when the door of his room was closed, my eyes suddenly grew moist. His behaviour broke my heart because I had not thought of going through such a torment again, mostly with him. I was then convinced that as I had come to France through a side door, I was paying a high price. I sat on the bed over an hour, crying softly. At about nine o'clock, Richard showed up again in my room and possessed my body at will, then returned to his own where he came out washed, dressed and ready to go to work. He invited me into the kitchen to have breakfast with him. I had no choice, so I joined him. He showed me where he kept spare keys in case I wanted to go out during his absence, and then he gave me some money and promised to call me during the day. His kindness, which contrasted with his insensitivity a few hours earlier, toned down my concern. So I made the effort to look less affected than I actually was.

It was as calm and smooth a day as I had seen for a long time. I turned around in Richard's huge apartment, not knowing what to do to keep myself busy. I called my parents and talked to my mother with a much calmer and rested voice, as she observed. I promised to send her money in a few days. For the first time I had the courage to admit that I had parted with George for over a year, but I deliberately did not give details because I did not want her to worry. I then told her that the other man I was in a relationship with was richer. Obviously, I avoided talking of my past job as she assumed I was still working and I could not tell her anything because the idea of hurting her, she who was so devoted to her parish and had worked so hard to educate us with Christian values, was unbearable. So I opted for a lie, but not too far from the truth because I did not want to be the cause of the introduction of the devil into her home that she continually inundated with divine praises and blessings. The truth, however cruel, of my life in France would have dealt a devilish blow that only my damnation and banishment from my family could have repaired. Her soft words actually begged me never to seek money, especially at the price of my body, which was a precious gift that I really had to respect. The memories of these words drew thick tears down my emaciated cheeks. I quickly had to interrupt our conversation. And, in any case, the joy brought about by my promise of a future Western Union was such that she could not notice my choked voice at the end of our discussion.

After several weeks, Richard and I were talking a little bit more of our past. He clearly told me that he was too self-interested to give the hope of a married life to any woman; he had tried to marry twice but his plans failed because his partners were too typical for him. He thought I was different and I could certainly succeed in satisfying his emotional instability because I had shown myself to be quite flexible and compliant, unlike his former girlfriends. He said he could make me no promises for the future. The only thing he advised me to do was to continue behaving myself and he would spoil me in return. His words were pacifying and his attention for me was quite extraordinary and far beyond anything I expected from a white man since my separation from George, because I ended up believing that white men despised Africans because they saw them as nothing but exotic objects of sexual perversion. My misfortune prescribed by George, followed by the lack of compassion of the clients I had met before

Richard had wrought in me a very negative image of those whom I now considered as perverse. Fortunately, Richard showed me just the opposite even though his compassion was selfish, which led me to share with him my confidences.

One evening, at his request, I narrated how George brought me to France and how later, he had cowardly pushed me into the infamous hands that isolated me all this time at the place he had encountered me. Discussing this mishap made me realize that this past had left a very bitter mark in my life because I was forever hurt. I almost confessed to him that George's souvenir still haunted me on a regular basis, and my morale was far from being as strong as it appeared, because my pain was much greater than I could show. Several times, when working for Jesabel, I was afraid never to get out, but fortunately, he had come as a breath of liberation, with his considerable humanity, and had transformed the vicious downward spiral that was now linked to my destiny, allowing me to get on with my life, as a free individual. For that reason I was very grateful to him.

Richard listened intently. His face looked devoid of feelings, which made me confused because I did not know what he thought of this experience. When I had finished, he admitted being a long-time friend of Jude. I became scared and suspicious: it was amazing and it explained to me why Jesabel had agreed to let me go with him! She could therefore continue to monitor me through him. I instantly thought that the floral bouquet life had given me through this deceitful benefactor was in fact a wreath for the funeral of my broken spirit. I was shaken by dread and I wanted to die. However, seeing my distress, unexpectedly, Richard added that Jesabel had often talked to him about me in rather glowing terms, because, despite the time spent under her roof, my behaviour had not changed as my misguided life had failed to make me become as nagging and combative as the other girls; instead I had remained extraordinarily serene. She had been thinking of getting rid of me for some time because I was a burden to her activities. She normally kept only newcomers in the building, to be trained before being relocated in the provinces or on the French-Swiss border where she had strong contacts. I thought of her, authoritarian and full of herself: her solid appearance was really hiding all the evil that was deeply rooted in her mind and urged her to try to harm as much as she had suffered. But, many girls eventually escaped despite the substantial resources she put in place to monitor them and to ensure she would always have a stock of renewed, young, deprived ladies, ready to work for her, sometimes willingly.

This was also how I learnt without surprise that Bridget was part of Jesabel's monitoring unit. I therefore concluded that her alleged friendship with me was intended only to teach me how to become an exemplary prostitute, sufficiently depraved by sex and misled by drugs. I was therefore de-lighted that something in me had resisted that programmed perversion, thus pushing Jesabel to sell me to Richard against her will. Such was my conclusion when he had finished his explanation about the way he had come to my studio. In this milieu where the meaning of deeds was implicit, every detail seemed unnecessary. I entreated Richard to spare me any fur-ther contact with Jesabel or her husband, because I longed to free myself from their memory.

I was relieved to hear him saying he did not see them fre-quently, and his encounters with Jude usually took place at the racetrack on some weekends when, together, they gam-bled until the last horse race. Moreover, he was suspicious about Jude's naive attitude because his sensitive and realistic look was in great contrast to the inexorable domination of his merciless wife whom he feared and followed like a faithful servant. He could not understand the relationship of that un-characteristic couple, who had been married for seven years, because Jude was always nervous when he was with Jesabel, and when she coughed, he was the one shivering. Also, to conceal his true personality, especially his weakness, and avoid the bad influence of his wife, he was drinking a lot, but not to the extent of getting completely drunk. Listening to Richard, it was clear he did not like Jesabel very much. Al-though he was inclined to continue his description of the strange pair, he had to interrupt our conversation to answer his phone. With one hand, he asked me to leave the lounge, which I obediently did.

During another discussion, I confessed that I continued taking the toxic pills Bridget had sold me before I left, but parsimoniously. Richard decided to send me to a rehab cen-tre. He refused to have an addict in his house. Therefore, the morning of my first appointment at the centre, he entered my room and methodically searched all four corners. He found the pills hidden in a plastic bag that was carefully buried in one of my shoes. Firm and inflexible, despite my pleas that I would keep my promise and never use them, he threw every-thing in the toilet, and then drove me to the centre in tears.

It took me over three months to be successfully weaned off the harmful product which I had been accustomed to for so many months but which had nevertheless given me dyna-mism and artificial well-being. However, it was not easy: of course I did not have to work as hard as before, but I became taciturn and my days passed usually without a hitch, which brought about a slight depression that increased gradually because I was distrustful for several weeks at the centre, so I refused to open my heart to anyone mainly owing to the fact that I had since learnt not to be charmed by sweet words that could blow away like the wind. But, since Richard was tracking my treatment closely, he had specifically asked for the monitoring of my psychological well-being.

They had given me a wonderful and patient psychologist who allowed me to express the daily difficulties of my new life, but especially my anxieties and my chronic insomnia. Thanks to persistent monitoring by this dynamic woman, I eventually found sleep again. Alas, her assistance did not last, because Richard thought that, four weeks later, I was strong enough to get by without her help. The lady, whose name was Hermine, asked Richard to let me pursue the programme to its completion. Without resistance, he yielded to the natural charm of her beautiful ebony face that was constantly enhanced by discreet make-up highlighting her generous lips. So, our meetings became weekly before finally stopping after three months, when Richard felt that because I no longer saw my exploiters this would prevent me having any relapse. Luckily, my therapist, who had taken pity on me from our first encounter, wanted to keep in touch with me. That was how I finally made my first real friend in France.

Short in stature, Hermine was always perched on stilettos matching her admirable retro-chic elegant outfits. She had such passion for her profession that she often managed to soften her patients quickly, gaining their confidence like she did with me. Being one of her favourites made me feel proud, so that I could no longer do without her resolute support, which gradually led me to stand back from my misadventures in order to better understand my future with Richard, but especially to regain my dignity, which, according to her, was up to me.

One day I went to our appointment. She was happy to see me.

"You're now looking good. Very well..." she said before greeting me while forming a wide smile.

"Yes, thanks to you," I replied, returning her smile.

"You think so? I'm not eating for you!"

"But you listen to me and help me get better…"

"You are solely responsible for your well-being… whatever you do, you're doing it for your own good, right? How does that affect me? Do not underestimate your own efforts. And let nobody make you believe that one day you will manage to do something in your life if you have no respect for yourself."

Although our conversation lasted an hour, it seemed too short. I went home feeling hungry, because Hermine's uplifting company always relieved me. Indeed, her positive impact gradually led me to give up drugs. Her words strengthened me and that chiefly freed me from my deep sense of guilt and remorse. In the end, my regrets were dispelled, giving way to new self-reliance.

Meanwhile, the quiet surroundings offered by Richard, who still slept in a different room, also revived my self-esteem. I felt I was coming back to life. I gained weight visibly, so I took that opportunity to send my family some pictures. Richard never gave me money, except when he believed that I deserved a reward for being good or for giving him great pleasure. And, as quickly as possible, part of that money ended up in the hands of my mother who was distributing it to other family members according to their respective needs of the moment. With the rest I bought myself a few little things I needed in the vicinity. I already knew how to use the subway, alone; I could go to a specific location, aimless, and come back. Richard taught me to know Paris through a map and revealed to me that I had lived in the eighteenth arrondissement during the time I had spent in custody. Using this map, I made sure to avoid that area of Paris when wandering about.

Those mornings I did not go to the rehab centre, when Richard had gone to work, I tried to read some books in his library, but often, I forced that idea out of my mind, because reading was not a natural activity at home. Back home, my parents never had enough money to pay for schoolbooks, let alone leisure books. And since there was no library in the high school I attended, I often contented myself with photo-stories found in the Ghanaian hairdresser's salon, or occasionally borrowed some books from a friend of mine whose parents were well-off enough to register her at the French Cultural Centre. Failing to read, instead I listened to the radio because I loved modern music, whereas Richard only had classical music. One day, by chance, I managed to catch a radio broadcast playing African music. Now I could also listen to news from my country when cleaning, ironing or cooking for the evening. Indeed, to the kill idleness, I had offered to take care of Richard's home, which also made me feel less guilty about enjoying his generosity. Thus, from time to time, I went to the supermarket to shop for home when Richard gave me money to that end. But more often, for my own particular needs, I used my money because I had once heard him bitterly criticizing a former relationship he had fed and housed for months, and who had left for another man. Although my condition in Richard's house was not different from a piece of furniture, my dignity was pushing me to participate financially with my small savings, the money I had earned in awkward circumstances. However, I was careful never to forget the important family responsibility that weighed on my shoulders and that I could not escape. As there was a beautiful big church on the way to the supermarket, I often popped in to admire its colourful roses and the altar divinely decorated with flowers of all colours. I liked to spend a few minutes to meditate and light a candle, because I always came out invaded with positive vibes. I observed this practice in secret, because Richard did not believe in God and I did not want to be thwarted in the one activity that brightened my deeply hurt conscience.

Most weekends were spent in Richard's cottage. It was an old house inherited from his parents and renovated to accommodate his friends during the summer or to relax over a weekend when he did not have to travel to Belgium, Switzerland or somewhere in France for businesses he never commented on. Richard was indeed a very busy man and enjoyed spending his money to excess. Sometimes it troubled me to compare his expensive lifestyle to the laborious life my family was experiencing in my country. In addition, our standard of living was very comfortable and there was no reason to have doubts about his business trips, although in my mind, his friendship with my former jailers called forth a few suspicions.

I had been living with my new master for six months. One day, he told me he would be travelling to Switzerland for a two-day business trip. He promised to call me on his arrival, but failed to do so. The next morning, when I returned from the centre, a message on my mobile phone informed me that he had arrived late at his hotel, had tried to call me but was unsuccessful because his room's phone did not work! Listening to this message, I laughed at myself thinking that, in fact, my childish face was certainly a picture of such impertinence that was now mixed with disrespect of the people I had rubbed shoulders with since my arrival in France, including Richard. Therefore, when he returned, it was useless to try to expose to him what I knew was a blatant lie. The way he lived his life was really questionable and made me believe that he probably was hiding more than I could imagine. Obviously, I was now definitely cynical and sceptical about his so-called business trips, which certainly enabled him to freely satisfy his thirst for new conquests, far from home. This mattered little, as long as I was not directly involved, it was bearable. In fact, being quick and intuitive, Richard had prepared to repair his lie by taking me to the restaurant that evening for an intimate dinner for two followed, as he determined, by meeting some of his friends I had never met.

Our dinner was pleasant and gave us another opportunity to discuss my situation in France. He looked genuinely concerned about my instability, so he promised to get my passport from Jesabel and see what he could do about it. The way he talked to me confirmed a gap between us, since he made it clear that it was out of question to live together as a couple. I then understood that he had removed me from one hell to put me in another, less hard: my status had not really changed, except that instead of serving multiple clients, I did only one. This sad reality opened my eyes when Richard took me to his friends whom he had previously praised for their kindness and gentleness. Once there I found I was to be swapped like a toy. So, that night I was offered to two strangers who possessed me without my consent, once again, after Richard had gone home.

When one of the two men politely took me back to Richard's door, pushing a wad of bills into the palm of my hand, he asked me if I had had a good time, as if my opinion would make a difference. Without answering back or looking at him, I opened the door with a bruised heart, a sense of betrayal that made me very angry. I walked into my room quietly. I took a quick shower, and then went to bed. I prayed that Richard remained in his because the hatred in my mind urged me to mutter insults against him, so I feared what I might do to him. Luckily, he stayed in his bedroom all night long and did not wake me to achieve the unavoidable morning ritual he had established between us since my first night in his apartment.

He did not give me money this time and promised to come back early enough to take me shopping and cook together. I did not reply, not daring to ask him questions about the experience he had put me through. He did not enquire about how things went, even if he had surely got a prior report from his allies. So both of us pretended nothing had happened. At my request, he agreed, however, to drop me at the post office to send money to my family.

That afternoon I called Hermine to relate what Richard had done to me. She told me to meet her at her office where I found her shortly after. Shocked by my account, she immediately became passionate.

"He's playing with you... it's obvious!" she said, revolted. "What a pity! And you, why do you take that... If you want it to stop, you'll have to make a decision..."

"Richard got me out Jesabel's prison, so..."

"So what? So... now you must be his slave?"

"No, I'm just grateful..."

"Grateful or submissive? You should know where you stand. And where is respect in all that? You think Richard truly respects you to get you out of Jesabel's clutches?"

I don't think so," I said anxiously.

"Do you think that this *gratitude* will earn you any affection from him? To him, you're nothing but some erotic thing... It makes me sick!"

Hermine was now very angry. I almost regretted confessing my lack of courage towards Richard. "How can you live like that?" She whispered as if I was not present before questioning me, "Tell me, have you ever said 'no' to him, at least once?"

"Hmm...?"

I was thinking aloud, hoping to find an example to contradict Hermine, but in vain. Faced with my silence, she added in a balanced voice, "Don't look for an answer... I know it. But let me tell you one thing: when I was your age, I loved to read. It helped me understand many things. Do you read?"

"No... only magazines..."

"Ha, Ha, ha," she chuckled bravely as if she was mocking me. "You, the young African women of today... reading, you don't want to. Going to school, you don't want to. But you believe that whites are the best solution to social change! Between those whitening their skin and those wear silly green or blue lenses, or those colouring their hair blond or even those like you whose personalities are completely erased before a white man... honestly, what's the world coming to? Let me tell you one thing: for Richard, you're black and will always be, so all the efforts you undertake to achieve *his* perfection will never be enough because his judgment is marked by intolerance."

"I'm not trying to be perfect for him..."

"I'm saying what I see, Yvette. Beware and listen carefully: searching perfection is not bad... but trying to be perfect to suit Richard's expectations is unhealthy. Let me also tell you that if you continue to let him undermine you like George, then you're destroying your moral values and culture. Look where you are today, just because you followed a white man you fell in love with over the Internet, but also because you chose to trust him blindly. True or false? Where is your dignity, Yvette, eh? I am sure that when you left your country for France, you couldn't envisage being hurt or fighting for your freedom. Am I wrong?"

She had obviously lost her professionalism, which surprised me because I was not expecting her scolding.

"No," I said shamefully.

Noticing my defeated look, Hermine rose and walked towards a shelf located behind her desk. She chose a book and came over to me, much calmer.

"You know, if you want to get out of your situation, you must start contemplating the world through the eyes of a black person, not with those of white people, because you can dress like them, eat like them, but your culture is different! Holding on to your African culture is your strength... You and I are responsible for our race, you know? Have you ever wondered why white people who go to Africa or in the Caribbean are treated like distinguished individuals? Are they strangers or not?"

"They are strangers..."

"So why are you, when you come to settle down in their country... why are you treated like an uncultivated, reckless lady? If I got angry... it wasn't against you because I understand you... but you can't continue living this way. Everything I said today is only to show you that you need to open your eyes... Stop romanticizing your relationship with Richard, because there isn't one! In any case, for Richard, you're an African, a black woman... he did not buy you from Jesabel because he loves *you*. He did it only for him and him alone and that's why you will never be cherished, no matter your efforts to please him! That's how it is, most of the problems you've had come from the colour of your skin, but chiefly from the way you perceive yourself: George used you to satisfy his sudden unhealthy interest in easy money, but above all and that's the worst, as Fanon said: he loves black women because his thoughts are as weird as those people who clearly display their hatred for our race; as regards Jesabel, she exploited you because of your naivety and your extreme trust in others. To me, she has lost her African identity and has blended in with the horrid mass of modern pro-slavers who justify their actions by their won sufferings. She's crazy, she needs help... Fortunately Richard came and released you anyway. But he's just the kind master who allows the slave to eat at his table, but in the evening he sneaks into her bed to rape her."

"You're surely right, Hermine," I replied almost sighing, because her observations saddened me.

I left dispirited, but not by what Hermine had said. She had never been tough with me before. I readily admitted that the passion and compassion that animated her were only for my good. Never had anyone, not even my parents, drawn my attention to such important facts. Indeed, when George came to the country, my family and I welcomed him like a royal to the best of our limited resources. All because we venerated his skin colour and secretly hoped that having a white man among us would lead us to a social change that my parents had expected for years. But what had happened once I set foot in the country of my alleged fiancé? From disappointment to rock bottom, George had destroyed our dreams. Yes, Hermine's analysis was pertinent: since I was in France, I had involuntarily moved from one person's control to another without growing personally. While I had refused to leave George, I had wanted to run away from Jesabel and her band, and now I was trying to settle with Richard who, at first, proved to have more respect for me than the first two. Hermine was right! I was behaving like a freed slave with her master: feeling indebted to him, she could not imagine herself opposing him for the outrage he was submitting her to. Most terrible was the fact that I was so attached to my recent past that the top of the steep hill I was trying to reach daily by submitting to Richard's selfish rules seemed more acceptable as I could continue to support my family back home.

For the first time that evening, I began to wonder what Richard expected of me: sometimes he inspected my daily activities like a jealous lover, so I had to answer many questions: what could a lady of my age be seeking outside when not working or not going to college? Had I met another man since living with him? Would I tell him if I did? Sometimes I took his enquiries for a game, well aware that each of us had to live our life independently, except that I was his and my body, his fount of pleasure, owed him and had to be available to him continually. Of course, he never expressed himself clearly, so I drew my own conclusions based on his mysterious attitude.

One weekend in mid-April, Richard decided that we would spend the day at home. As I was not feeling well, he cooked the lunch all alone. Later, he began his little games of love that I usually resisted to excite him more. But that day, I was tired and did not want to be touched. Frustrated and angry, he grabbed my arm vigorously.

"I forbid you to reject me, you understand?" he said in a thundering tone.

This incident made me realize with regret that, despite his civility, Richard never showed his feelings. It was the first time I had seen his temperamental irritation. I was deeply disturbed, so I asked him to forgive me, and then I took off my clothes to comply with his desire, which half an hour later earned me the reward of a few Euros that did not console me about his refusal to consider my wishes.

In the evening, he did not enter his bedroom immediately as usual, but sat in the living room for a long time where he smoked a cigar that made the whole house smell awfully. I watched him quietly through my ajar door, until I fell into sleep. The next morning, he transgressed his routine by not turning up in my room. When I joined him in the kitchen for breakfast, I was surprised to read remorse in his eyes. He did not speak to me... His disgraceful demeanour was still printed in his head and visibly annoyed him. So I tried to calm things down by narrating the atrocities that I gone through to make him understand that his reaction was not the worst I had experienced. He listened religiously and when I had finished speaking, for the first time since I had lived with him, Richard got up from his chair and kissed me. His unexpected affection brightened my eyes that overflowed with tears of joy.

X

In the days that followed, the atmosphere of the house changed. Richard was more charitable than in the past. He appealed to an acquaintance, a lawyer, to start a process to rectify my illegal status. I was very pleased because with a residence permit, I perceived a solution for gaining my independence. Although very attached to Richard despite everything, I was determined not to stay with him if I ever managed to get my residence permit.

I met the lawyer several times to provide him with the information he needed to file my application with immigration. I did not have much to say because I did not want to reveal my sad past through my mouth. But Richard had already given him a reasonable account to save me that humiliating ordeal. What he wanted from me was documents that would support my application, but I did not have any: for over three years living in France, I had moved from greedy hands to unhealthy ones. I did not have any evidence of my stay throughout this time, except for the customs stamp in my passport, which proved my entry into the territory. The lawyer was shocked and enquired whether, at least, I had been sick and gone to a hospital. He found it hard to believe me when I said that when confined in Jesabel's building, all diseases were taken care of by the governess. My file was so incomplete! Despite that, we submitted my request to the police headquarters. My lawyer was utterly uncertain about the outcome and advised me not to expect anything.

During the following months, my life with Richard took a more cheerful turn. He did not loan me to his friends to embellish their libertine evenings. Similarly, his informal trips strangely stopped. We spent a lot of time together when he was not working. He even took great care to teach me the history of France and shared with me his knowledge about the various aspects of French daily life. When I was alone, still not being patient enough to read, I continued to educate myself through television and some educational games that Richard taught me to love. However, despite this growing familiarity, we still did not share the same bedroom.

This closeness lasted about four months and time seemed only to emphasize it. One day I found out that I was pregnant. Richard was indifferent when I broke the news to him. I was not surprised because he was concerned about the welfare of others only when his own interest was served. From that moment I knew that all his behaviour was only pretence. A few days later he told me he would check me in for my abortion: he did not want children! Inwardly I hurried to complete his thought: "...certainly not with a woman picked in a brothel!" As I hoped this pregnancy could weigh favourably in my application and solve the problem of my residence permit, I expressed my refusal with delicacy. Richard had a calm character bordering slyness. He said nothing of course, because for him, his decision was final. In order to change his mind, I returned to the lawyer, who confirmed that having a child by Richard would surely be a good addition to my file. He therefore advised me to see a doctor to get a pregnancy certificate. When I informed Richard of what I was planning to do, he objected. Not even a month later, I received a summons to attend an interview at the immigration department through my lawyer.

My appointment was at nine o'clock in the morning. Thinking that I would be received as soon as I got there, I was outside the huge immigration building half an hour in advance. What a great surprise to see a line of over one hundred people waiting patiently to be allowed within the premises. I joined the queue. After ten minutes, thinking that my notice might exempt me from this inappropriate queuing, I walked to the nearest police officer posted and asked permission to enter because the time of my appointment was getting close. With his forefinger he showed me the people lining, saying they had also been summoned for the morning. I then returned to my previous position which had been taken by newcomers. I told them that I was behind an Asian man who served as a witness to regain my place in the queue. As time progressed, the multi-ethnic line dwindled in front of me while it stretched out behind. Men and women of all colours, sometimes accompanied by one or more children were moving patiently under a slight autumnal coldness that refrigerated our legs which were already stiffened from the standing position. I could not feel my hands or the tips of my ears anymore; and fine droplets began to flow from my similarly frozen nose.

When I was about to begin my second hour of waiting, my legs went totally numb and my back became painful because of my condition. At last, I came before a security guard who showed me the security scanner for me to drop my bag and my coat. I passed through a metal gate and then I took my belongings. Not knowing exactly where the office mentioned on my notice was, I took the same direction as those in front of me.

I now found myself in a large hall where the receptionist, a very friendly white lady, gave me a number and directed me to the first application service area. A dozen silent people were sitting there, all waiting to be called by their number. When my turn came, about an hour later, I walked to the counter with great anxiety. A black lady whose skin was so clear that you would have thought she was mixed race received me. Her skin was so smooth that I found it suspicious.

Therefore I took advantage of the moment she was reading through my documents to steal a look at the folds of her hands, searching for any trace of blackish spots betraying the use of bleach. But the skin of her hands was as uniform as her face. She was now looking at me. I was embarrassed about my attitude but fear took over again in my mind. She asked me some questions about my situation. As I had been prepared by my lawyer, I answered as much as I could. Our interview was not very long. She went to consult a manager. After a few minutes that seemed longer than an hour, she returned to her desk where I was leaning on one elbow.

"Application inadmissible!" she said dryly.

As my face betrayed my lack of understanding, the lady continued, "Your application has been rejected, "she said without looking at me, while writing something on a document she handed me after.

"Please sign here," she told me, giving me a pen and showing me where I had to write my name.

I quickly browsed the document. It was their request that I leave the French territory within two months, otherwise I would be expelled! I signed it. Then the next second, I reviewed this moment that was marking the beginning of a new descent into hell: I was now officially illegal. Indeed, in the morning, since I had woken up, the coldness of my body, pain, the endless wait and finally, nothing. My ears were no longer able to hear one word of advice the lady later gave me. I left the premises of the immigration department at a fast pace with my unpleasant invitation in hand. In my head, only one desire: going home as quickly as possible to take refuge in my bedroom.

I went back home. I pushed bitter tears away with all my strength. I really had a lump in my throat, but it was useless to cry: I expected it a bit since the lawyer had prepared me for this. However, the hope and faith that had accompanied me at immigration had vanished. What was I going to do now? I began to think that if my lawyer was an African, probably I would have been better equipped to handle that situation. Did my case mean something to Richard's lawyer? His interests were different from mine, but especially from those of his friend, so he might have missed one or more important things a fellow African would have seen or used more effectively in my file. My mother! How appalled she was going to be when she heard of my eviction notice. I decided not tell her right away, because it would have been particularly painful for her to live with the constant fear of me landing back home without notice, after a possible police check that would have shortened my stay in France. I was going to fight for my future child, but also for my family! Thus I spent the rest of the day until my partner's return: asking myself questions, doubtful, and mistakenly accusing my lawyer.

Richard seemed almost as disappointed as me. However, not taking my case personally, that evening he insisted on taking me out to a restaurant to clear my mind. I had to wear an elegant dress while my blood was stirring up and, one by one, all my limbs were clenched. I did not need a meal. I needed a residence permit! Then I told myself that I would never understand the mentality of white people. For us, such a circumstance would have led to prolonged discussions and meetings to find a solution, even if it could ultimately prove futile. But certainly not a meal in town... How would food ease my mind?

I followed Richard reluctantly and not convinced that his intention to please me would soften my frustration for the rest of the day. He told me we were going to a place that would make me a little more joyful, at least for a short time. We were soon to arrive in a trendy neighbourhood where he parked his car. Walking beside me, he stopped before a modest storefront door he pushed open to allow me to enter first. Some soft African music was putting rhythm into the calm and harmonious atmosphere of a unique broad room, illuminated by small lamps set in between tribal masks. All around the room, scattered tables were decorated with tablecloths matching the same African fabrics hanging along the windows. Fascinated, for one minute I was transported to my country. I completely forgot about Richard who brought me back to reality by patting my shoulder and asking me to move forward.

A young woman showed us to a table in a corner of the room, although we had the choice since it was not packed. Shortly after, another lady, older, came to greet us in a way so familiar that Richard was forced to admit that he used to regularly come to this place with Jesabel and Jude long ago. When the lady left us, he added that, in the basement was a second room that opened after midnight. As I saw no access to the cellar, I did not believe him; hence he suggested we stayed beyond midnight, so I could see for myself.

Each of us ordered a dish: I chose a braised tilapia and Richard got meat brochettes that we ate with slices of fried plantain. All this reminded me of my mother's cooking and, with nostalgia, I recalled the time, long ago, when my family got together for royal feasts for first communions or weddings, now replaced by funerals that drew more hungry people than distressed ones. Richard had never been to Africa but knew it from his readings and his many African acquaintances. He had already heard about the feasting and drinking that occurred during post-burial repasts, which he said was ridiculous given the money the bereaved families had to squander. Richard truly tried to make me enjoy myself that night, so I forgot my fears for some time.

After dinner, we remained at our table, quietly observing our neighbours who were sharing their conversation with the entire place as they were talking very loudly, regardless of our presence. They were actually discussing the burning issue of living illegally, which upset any chance of me feeling fully at peace as the atmosphere of the restaurant was supposed to bring me. Nevertheless, I was a bit relieved by the idea that I was not alone in this situation, but I felt much disturbed to realize that the primary concern of my African compatriots in France was their residence status. Eventually, midnight came. The restaurant, which was almost empty by then, revived because its basement was about to unveil its secrets.

The manager, an African woman of about fifty wearing a beautifully embroidered long *gandoura*, invited the last customers who were still dining to hurry to leave because the law forbade her to open beyond that time. Some had their leftovers packed; others immediately took the exit door, not without complaining from the outside where the boss had to follow them to ask them to tone it down so as not to disturb the residents. Meanwhile, the regulars, like Richard of course, whom I followed, went down a staircase hidden behind the counter which led to the middle of a small, round room, comfortably furnished with tables and lamps, which gave the whole place an intimate cocoon-like light. Richard and I sat down in front of the stairs were we could easily watch the movements of incoming customers. Most of them were men, which seemed bizarre.

After half an hour came a group of joyful young beauties, dressed in a flirty way and who looked undoubtedly less old than me. They were all Africans and seemed to have affinities with the regulars who offered a glass to one or the other. At our table, silence was more eloquent than Richard: I understood and he knew it. Euphoria seized almost the entire back-room when some girls began to outline suggestive dance steps to the musical sounds out of a moderate, imperceptible audio system. I now feared I would be forced to take part in a performance that would have sent me back to my recent and sorrowful past. I begged Richard to take me home. He did not answer, got up without hesitation and started off towards the exit.

The return journey was shorter. When we got home, in a laconic voice, I thanked Richard for the evening, and to avoid any comments or suggestion from him, I added that I was tired, hoping he would understand I was in no mood to talk, let alone have him in my room. I closed the door behind my heels because darkness had resurfaced in my mind. Even the simple enjoyment Richard expected me to experience would have almost turned into a nightmare if I had not intervened in time: my memories of the past had left a heavy mark on my life as a woman and I did not know how to behave normally again, since my period of captivity continued to haunt me and afflict me during intimate moments. I needed comfort; my partner did not know how to give me that.

I could not help thinking that vice was unquestionably stuck on my skin! I began to believe that someone had cast an evil spell on me so that I would never be happy in France. Perhaps my place was not in this country after all. Perhaps it was simply time to confess to my family that the France we imagined, or that some people were telling us about when they returned home with suitcases packed with gifts, that France had not smiled at me. And, to my greatest misfortune, the one that had welcomed me had a hateful face. I spent all night awake, meditating and weeping. The lie, the silence in which I got bogged down, the betrayal of my family and my own values... was all that worth it? I had hoped for a comfortable life to get my family out of poverty, but nothing ever let me predict the dishonour I was plunged into and that I somehow finally accepted. On the one hand, I felt guilty for letting George push me into my own debauchery, because from the moment I understood that he no longer wanted me, and despite my confirmed doubts and his sudden authoritarian attitude, I did nothing. On the other, I now thought it necessary to free myself from the vicious circle of lies and of all the memories associated with George by revealing the truth to my parents. I was somewhat reassured by the idea that their pity for my poor fate would help me overcome the throes of my humiliation. For that reason, I told myself that the only practical alternative was to face this situation and that I had to find a way to get by, with or without Richard. So a solution had to emerge by sunrise, otherwise, I was determined to call my parents because it was better for me to return home rather than to continue to undergo this degrading depravity, despite Richard's visible efforts to make it substantially less abominable. The secret had become too heavy and my psychological health precarious. I could not go on like that.

XI

Dawn found me sitting on the bed with a puffy face while my body was afflicted with the weariness that weighed upon my shoulders. Moreover, a severe headache made me very irritable. I needed someone. I was powerless; I put my hand on my warm stomach. I was carrying life in me.

Richard came in at about seven o'clock, as usual. My pathetic state led him to ask me many questions. Several weeks had gone without him asking anything about my pregnancy. My recurring exhaustion did not bother him either. It was not his problem, as long as I continued to satisfy his libido.

I did not answer him all the time he questioned me. When he had finished speaking, I tried to explain that I had no reason to expect any improvement in my condition after everything I had experienced until now. My pitiful voice thanked him for his good intentions for letting me live in his house, which was really the only positive thing that had happened to me since I had left George. But could I go on serving him without thinking about my own well-being? That was why I had decided to keep the baby, especially since I had the assurance that by having this child, I could easily get a residence permit. Basically, I was ready to part with him, so I hoped that by these words, when the time came, he would not be surprised. Feeling very indebted to him for removing me from the hands of greedy Jesabel, I decided to inform him of my plans rather than running away, but especially to enable him to find a solution, if there was any at all, before my final decision.

Richard did not expect to hear me talking like that. He was still attentive to the end. When I stopped talking, he promised to give me an answer in the evening after work. He immediately went out of my bedroom, evasive. A few minutes of silence blew around the house, and then I heard his voice from his bedroom. The corridor which separated our rooms usually did not allow any communication or indiscretion of this kind. So I guessed that he was yelling or screaming on the phone. But I was too exhausted from my sleepless night, so I could not catch a word of what he was saying. After half an hour, I heard a distant "goodbye" announcing that he was leaving the house.

Alone, lying on my bed, I let myself be lulled by the calm atmosphere. Finally, torpor plunged me into a deep sleep that lasted until mid-afternoon. I hastened to cook the dinner so I could be ready for a further discussion with Richard when he came back. Then I called my mother. I told her I was pregnant, but I did not know how long because I still had not gone to the hospital. The joy of this news made her cry, while on my side, I was weeping over my fate. I omitted to mention my eviction, since Richard's decision would be crucial for my future. I was both excited and nervous because Richard was very unpredictable and he did not like his plans to be disrupted. The serenity he had shown in the morning was also very disconcerting. In addition, the day went by too quickly as a prediction of what I should expect. I tried to listen to my body all day long, hoping a sign would prepare me for what my partner would hold for me, but in vain. By the time I had finished cooking my anxiety was unbearable, so I called Hermine who was at the centre I had stopped going to for over a month. As she was aware of my illegal circumstances, she helped me put things into perspective when I told her about my fear to go out now or even to stay at home as the mere fact of living at the address provided in my application to the immigration worsened my apprehensions.

"Only Richard can help you!" she exclaimed spontaneously.

"How?"

"You're expecting his child, right? I can assure you that this may be the key to your future in France... you understand?"

"Not really!"

"Since Richard has been using you... it's your turn to use him!"

"What do you mean?"

"Thanks to your pregnancy, if you leave him now, social services should look after you..."

"In my situation?"

"Exactly... your pregnancy can get you out of trouble, dear..."

"I don't understand."

"You will not be deported in your state... and Richard can help you if he recognizes the child is his," she said simply as if it was an obvious fact.

Then my only confidante went into an explanation of the procedures I should follow to get Richard to help me. When we finished our conversation, I began to pray to my God to make Richard merciful towards me, once more, and to incline his heart in the direction of my desires: letting me go because I had enough savings to live on in the beginning. In any case, speaking with my friend calmed me, even strengthening my intention to envisage the future from the best angle, with or without Richard. I was determined to talk to him.

Richard returned immediately after work. I tried to read his mood on his face. He was as emotionless as the other days. My heart was pounding but I struggled to remain serene. He served himself a drink and sat before the television, silent just like in the morning. Shortly after, he invited me to join him. I did, taking all my time and approaching like a servant ready to bow to her master. He made a movement with his hand to tell me to sit beside him. I obeyed. Without turning towards me, he said he had discussed my situation once again with the lawyer. His voice was low and sluggish. He took his time choosing his words, recalling our first meeting. I felt my pulse racing when suddenly the idea of my redemption from Jesabel for a price I did not know yet came to my mind, and like George, he would probably want to be refunded. Nevertheless, I was listening, staring at the black screen of the television he had turned off as soon as I sat down. In a few long minutes, he depicted a picture of my sad life without reproach in his voice. After that, he mentioned my satisfactory ability to quickly adapt to his way of life. I was confused, because until then, he had not once turned his eyes in my direction. After some time, he said he would marry me before the birth of the child, only to allow me to remain in France. Moreover, he ensured that I understood that even when married, our relationship would not change. I was so relieved because he had avoided me confronting him. I burst into tears, which prevented me from thanking him. Later, when we had dinner, I indeed expressed my appreciation, which he welcomed with his characteristic distance.

The next day I called Hermine who was unmoved by this turnaround from Richard.

"Richard marrying you!?" she shouted.

"That's what he said…"

"It is rather surprising for someone who doesn't want to start a family, right?"

"He emphasized that it was *only* to allow me to remain in France."

"Ah, I see…"

"What?"

"Well, the white lord has decided to maintain his black mistress… calculated anticipation!"

"I don't get it…"

"Well, I was talking to myself," she said evasively. "And you, what do you think of his proposal?"

"If this can help me with my situation…"

"What?" she said angrily. "You remember what I told you about your dignity? Here you react exactly like a disgraced slave in front of her white master. Yvette, if you want things to change, you must turn down the natural alienation within which Richard is trying to lock you *only* because you're living with him and depend on him. Take heart, and move on!"

"You're right," I said without conviction.

I really wished for a positive change in my life. However, back home, my family was counting on me. Leaving Richard abruptly would have affected them more than Hermine could imagine. That's why I never told her about all the money I was sending them regularly, as I imagined her blaming me for setting up their financial dependency. Also, shortly after our dialogue, I phoned my mother to tell her that Richard and I were getting married. The so much desired God's blessing had finally fallen on our family. She reminded me that before the ceremony, my fiancé would absolutely have to discharge his dowry duty for the family to approve of our wedding. As she did not know the details of my life, I promised to talk to Richard as soon as possible. He had never tried to be close to my family and refused to talk to my parents every time I phoned them in his presence. On those occasions, I had to invent pretexts to excuse his action. So, telling him of our traditions when he was disobeying his own principles only to prevent me from having to return to my country? It was unwise. The money I had saved, my pocket money and that kept after shopping for home, was going to be enough. And, anyway, that money came from Richard and I was going to send it to my family as his dowry.

I had to wait four months after the birth of our son for Richard to legally recognize him. Nothing changed at home despite his birth, just as Richard had warned me when he found that my pregnancy was too advanced to consider abortion. He continued to live his life in his room and me in mine that I shared with Emmanuel. Richard had refused to let him bear his surname, so I named him and chose his first name to express my gratitude to Heaven for having sent him to get me out of my illegal status because I relied more on him than on the promised marriage we no longer mentioned. Apart from his olive skin and straight nose inherited from his father, everything in him, from his full and well-designed lips to the tuft of curly hair flowing on his forehead and hiding his small ears, reminded me of my little sister as a child. He had a little, angelic, chubby face that filled me with strength. I was resolved to always protect him. Besides, because Richard was kind enough to hire a cleaning lady to look after the house twice a week, I had lots of time to spend with my son. So I took him to the park when the weather permitted or to church to pray to the Lord for his father to acknowledge him one day. Indeed, Richard never mentioned him. When he entered my room, less frequently than before, he would cast a quick glance towards his cot, engage in the task he had come for, and then return to his own bedroom.

The following month, I asked my parents to gather the family and establish the list of what was required for the dowry, but also to free them from this obligatory ritual. In fact, disregarding this ceremony could have fuelled a destructive animosity within the entire family, as this part of our tradition was immutable, so much so that one of my parents could even be killed for marrying their daughter without offering food to the family. Worse, I did not want the news of my son's birth to spread before the rite, to avoid seeing the dowry amount double or triple.

While I was busy with my family behind Richard's back, one evening he came from work whistling, a cigar in hand, and in a beaming mood. Instead of heading to his room or to the living room as he usually did, he came to mine. I was both curious and excited, thinking he had thought of me to share what was making him so happy. I asked him to put his cigar out because of the sleeping child, which he did willingly. He asked me to get ready for an outing. My heart leapt with joy instantly, because Richard had not shown any emotion towards me since I had forced him to have a child. As he had become more superficial than before, it was difficult to know what was in the back of his mind or identify his real needs. At first, I wanted to understand his motivation to take me for a walk. I speculated that time, my persistence and my refreshed enthusiasm since the birth of our child had softened him. Suddenly I thought of Emmanuel. Richard told me not to worry, since he was staying at home with him. I frowned suspiciously. His slightly whispered voice added that he had promised his friends that I would join them; also, he would take care of the baby. I looked at Richard defeated by disappointment. He could not stand the hate expressed by my eyes and left my room. In fact, my partner was a man of experience and had assets that were certainly very harmful and destructive, and he could continue to humiliate me as he wished. That was why he made sure that his sordid and coward schemes made my life at his house both peaceful and despicable. And above all, he did not seem to realize he was hurting me. In fact, I did not have the ability to anticipate or invalidate his injurious actions. The emotional pain Richard had just dug into my mind was deep. I owed him so much, and especially thanks to our child, I was granted a temporary residence permit. Despite the grief triggered by my inner struggle, I had no strength to get out of his trap. I stood up, got dressed, because I could not say no.

The next day, though my night was short because of the party organized by Richard's friends who swapped me in turns to satisfy their whims, I left the house early. I had hardly seen my partner since I came back late and he did not come into my room. I only heard the door slamming when he went to work. As my son was still asleep, I gently wrapped him in a cloak to go to the nearest post office to send money to my mother for my dowry which amounted to one thousand five hundred Euros.

When back home, signs of distress were obvious on my face. I knew I could no longer continue to live in a relationship that was held together only by my will. But mostly, I had no more strength to endure any further physical or mental torture. Also, for the sake of my son, it was time to change the course of this recurrent discomfort resulting from the accumulation of past frustrations, and Richard's deceptive way of living. Furthermore, for Emmanuel too, it was now imperative for me to preserve my psychological balance. To do this, I had to re-establish order in my life. I spent the day thinking about the path I had accomplished, emotionally and socially. No satisfactory answer came to ease my spiritual wounds that continued to bleed briskly. However, I was now convinced that only two directions were open to me. Not only was it high time I stopped focusing on the worst, but also I needed to make a decision. I was determined not to accept the things I disliked and that undermined me every day or worsened my resentment and denial of my suffering because of the influence of charismatic Richard.

Three days later, I called my mother early in the morning. It was a day of celebration for my family. My parents had expected this moment so much that their speech had been ready for a long time. The preparations started; my mother also apologized for having to shorten our discussion. I promised to call her later. However, the idea of going through this day far away from my family aroused more bewilderment in my thoughts darkened by the whirlwind marriage that I had brought about back home without the groom knowing. When he came to meet me soon after, he immediately noticed my deep contemplation and wanted to know what was happening. I could not tell him that my family was about to celebrate our traditional union with pomp. Instead, faced with my inability to speak, he deduced that my condition was due to a bit of homesickness. I nodded to agree with him, still looking quite distant. He was very courteous and returned to his room, without taking possession of my body. His gesture revived my courage, because things could actually improve between us.

Later, I was ashamed of my lack of courage. After all, I knew Richard was not a bad man. But his own fears had sometimes brought him to lead a very unbalanced life. Basically, he was the only person who had really helped me so far, and for that my respect for him was huge.

After Richard's departure, the cleaning lady came. As she started cleaning the house, I locked myself in my bedroom. I was frustrated and nervous. I wanted to think without any other presence but my child. He slept soundly throughout the morning, so I had to wake him to feed and change him. I was also relieved that his torpor stopped me from transferring my emotional unsteadiness to him. This state lasted until mid-afternoon, when I realized I had spent most of the time on the bed too, without doing anything. I left the bedroom when the maid took leave. It was now around two o'clock. I then dragged myself to the bathroom where I took a quick shower. After that, Emmanuel being awake, I also bathed him and dressed him in a lovely blue sky full-length slip, then slowly brushed his curly hair. Never had his tanned complexion been so radiant. My son was whiter than he was black! But I loved him! After his meal he fell asleep again, so I laid him in his bed. My phone rang. I answered. It was Richard who was worried about how I spent the day and promised to come back earlier. I reassured him and thanked him for his thoughtfulness and hung up as soon as he stopped talking.

A few minutes later, I called my mother. Her thanking words articulated with euphoria were a huge relief to me: the family council had approved Richard's dowry. However, this news did not cheer me up, as, more than six thousand miles away, my family was eating and drinking copiously so that the course of my life continued as it was, in submission. Suffering as a consequence of my lies and my family's total ignorance of what was going on, I was shattered. But part of my mission was accomplished! When I hung up the phone, I walked into my room. The first thing I saw when entering was Emmanuel's big eyes. He was lying on his stomach. He babbled and smiled when I approached his cradle. I took him in my arms. His warmth came over me. Life had given me love and light, which, all of a sudden, cast so much brightness on me that the sun started shining inside my heart. Emmanuel's comforting affection opened my eyes. I was no longer alone! My decision was instantaneous. I took all the money I had without counting it, put my key on the dresser, and carrying my son, I took the exit door.

Epilogue

All that happened long ago. Very long ago. I never left the accommodation the social services had provided me. As for Emmanuel, he was just offered a room on campus. I had not thought of this story for years. But this morning I received a letter. I opened it. A tear raced down my cheek. I quickly wiped it off.

After leaving Richard, driven by Hermine, I could resume my studies and got a degree. Today I work as a consultant for a humanitarian organization. My task is not always easy, since I coach the return home of young undocumented Africans arrested by the police. Most often refuse to leave, because of shame and because their families rely on them. I know that feeling well. And assisting others has allowed me to overshadow my own story, until this letter came. What will I tell Emmanuel? I have never told him about my past. The only thing he knows of his father is his name. However, he is his sole heir!

About the author

Régine Mfoumou was born in 1972 in Cameroon. She arrived in France in 1985 where she continued her studies until obtaining a Master's Degree in American civilization and a Doctorate (PhD) in English literature in 2001 at the Université la Sorbonne Nouvelle (Paris). As a Language teacher but also as a writer and translator, she has published many books in Paris, including historical literature and a political essay. *Descent into Hell in the Land of Human Rights* is his first novel.

Written to edify African youth worldwide, this book aims to explore immigration through its often overlooked mishaps. The story and characters have been constructed for this purpose, so any resemblance is purely coincidental.